LETTERS TO THE EDITOR

LETTERS TO

THE EDITOR

Mo McDonald

The Book Guild Ltd

First published in Great Britain in 2018 by
The Book Guild Ltd
9 Priory Business Park
Wistow Road, Kibworth
Leicestershire, LE8 0RX
Freephone: 0800 999 2982
www.bookguild.co.uk
Email: info@bookguild.co.uk
Twitter: @bookguild

Typeset in Adobe Garmond Pro

Printed and bound in Great Britain by CPI Group (UK) Ltd, Croydon, CR0 4YY

ISBN 978 1912362 943

British Library Cataloguing in Publication Data.
A catalogue record for this book is available from the British Library.

To my husband, Richard, my rock.

JACK

The paragraph was not quite right and I struggled for the word to conclude it.

'Go away, woman!' I shouted.

From the corner of my eye, annoyingly, I noticed Hannah's name light up on my iPhone. The ringtone was on silent but the vibrator made it hop slightly, in an irritating electronic way. I held it in my right hand, undecided whether or not to answer, as my thumb slid across the answer tab.

'Jack, can you talk? I must speak to you.'

'What's up? I'm in the middle of a chapter and the publisher is banging on about the deadline.'

'Do you remember Marian?'

'Marian?'

'Yes, Marian Davies. The woman you had a bit of a thing with.'

'Eh, I don't know, did I?'

'Yes, it all got nasty and—'

1

'Marian Davies! What about her? Why would I remember her after all this time?'

'Because, Jack, I think the past is coming to haunt you and you need to be ready.'

I laughed at this.

'Haunt me, what on earth do you mean? Hannah, what are you on about?'

'I have just been on Twitter and then on Facebook and your name is being passed around in a frenzy. You don't use social media, do you?'

'No, I do not. I keep my distance from all that stuff. What's that got to do with Marian? I don't understand. Is she on there about me? Don't get me involved in any messaging; I learned my lesson years ago. Fan mail is for my agent to deal with.'

'It's not her, it's her fifteen-year-old-granddaughter, Heather.'

'Why, what am I to her? I can hardly remember the bloody woman, let alone know her granddaughter!'

'She is saying that she got some files from Marian to help with her baccalaureate papers and she realised that you and Grandma had a falling out back in '84. She's doing what all youngsters do, sharing her findings online.'

'So why tell me? There's nothing for me to concern myself about, Hannah, so why mention it?'

'Because, from what I gather, Marian kept a detailed account and I think that you ought to be aware that you're going to be pestered by journalists knocking down your door, trying to get you to answer some tricky questions.' Hannah sounded stern in her warning.

'Young Heather has found it a surprise that her grandma has a past and that you featured in it. She probably thinks it's acceptable to tweet about a skeleton in the cupboard from so long ago. To her, the last century is history. I just feel that you need to be on your guard and don't answer the phone even. Not until you reflect on what went on with you and dear old Grandma. You are respected; Jack, you have become a national treasure and reputation is paramount, especially with all the investigations into the men of your age from the celebrity culture. A story like this will be seized on as another exposé. So, heed my words.'

'This all seems very odd and you are making a fuss about nothing, surely? I don't see how there is anything to worry about, really I don't.'

'Jack, I'm telling you, if this gets taken up by the media, you will be roasted alive. I beg you to take it seriously and think about what you are likely to be confronted with. Pauline is away, isn't she? Please take a couple of hours to think it through before you are approached – and believe me, you will be approached.'

'Erm, well if you think so. You've been my PA for as long as I can remember. I take your point. What do you suggest?'

'Stay home, ignore any callers and go through your archived correspondence. I filed and dated everything in A–Z in box files and they are stacked on the top two shelves in your study. Go through it regarding Marian. You need to be ready by the morning with confident answers to the awkward questions that will be fired at you once the news channels get buzzing from the tweets.'

'Okay, I suppose so. If you say so. You have been my Florence Nightingale thus far.' I gave a nervous laugh.

'So much for a quiet evening to write my novel. You'd better be right about this or no bonus for you this year for wasting my time, old girl.'

'Trust me, Jack. This is serious stuff.'

I ended the call by reassuring her that I would leave my paragraph unedited so as to find the necessary box file. I wasn't too keen on attempting the task she had set, but I trusted her judgement because she always had my best interests at heart. Hannah had been with me from the very beginning, taking care of my diary and replying to my correspondence. I am one of those dinosaurs who resist the instant communication of the modern world, employing Hannah to carry out secretarial skills on my behalf.

Back in the millennium plus fifteen, I received a lot of mail congratulating me on the great job I had done in bringing the Arts to such a wide BBC audience. Previously, it had only been aimed at, what had been perceived as, a privileged few. Going through the memorabilia from my TV programme, *The Show of Shows* and in amongst the many boxes of fan mail, I found what I was looking for. It was a bundle marked 'Marian Davies'. I had kept various devoted fans' letters, as many writers do, per chance posterity required it. Being a writer is my true vocation, dating a long time back to the days before I left Ireland. I am a writer; broadcasting gave me the bread and butter, but words were my true vocation. My passion for the written word started as a boy, long ago.

I looked at my watch; it was 5pm so I decided to make

myself a mug of coffee before settling down to read through the old correspondence. I was surprised how seeing her writing brought back the memory of her and how close we had been. I had also kept a diary of current affairs, along with my reaction to her comments, so I allowed my memory to wander back over the years between 1979 and 1983 with ease. I didn't have a clear picture in my head of what she looked like, though; time had squeezed that almost from my mind.

JACK

As I said, *The Show of Shows* finished in 2015, I was happy to end my career as a broadcaster in Britain on a high. The plan now was to finish my latest novel before starting a new career as a TV host in New York, so time was pressing and I didn't want bother from any silly gossip. But I knew better than to ignore the warnings of my trusted confidante, Hannah. So, as I sat at my desk about to plough through the old correspondence, I noticed the day's post unopened in a pile in front of me. On opening a handwritten envelope, I was taken by surprise yet again. It read as follows:

Dear Jack,

I read the articles and the many congratulations that the press has awarded you upon your farewell, before venturing to pastures new abroad. I would like to add my thanks for the unforgettable experience that you afforded me too. I spotted that you said that every single person who had ever been involved in your programme was responsible for the success of the award-winning series and also every artist who had ever been included. It made me wonder where I ought to send the invoice, for my contribution to the programme?

Kind regards,
Marian

I picked the letter up and read it through several times, feeling bemused and a little shocked as I hadn't received a letter from Marian for what seemed about thirty years. I recognised her handwriting immediately and assumed it was a joke – but was it? We'd had a long, intense relationship back in the early years of the programme and I didn't know whether there was a sense of menace there or not. I put the letter in my pocket to consider later. It would be no easy task winning an American viewing public, but it was a new challenge that I looked forward to and I wanted to draw a line under my past without allowing any skeletons to come out of any cupboards. If an intention to blackmail was being threatened, going through the memorabilia from the programme would indeed be of great importance. And was the plan for the timing to coincide with the granddaughter's tweet?

I returned to the bundle marked "Marian Davies"; as ever, Hannah had been very efficient. The editing room was as far as my technological expertise lay, so she had not scanned and copied such things, knowing my desire to move to social media was negligible. I mused over Marian's meaning in her letter and as I read through the old correspondence, dating back to the early eighties, it again brought back the memory of her and how intense things had been.

I turned to the very first communication from her, comparing notes in my diary from that time, too. I always have been like a trainspotter, using my writer's notebook to comment in, like a detective, just in case. Hannah had numbered each piece of correspondence in red ink enclosed in a circle, making my task easy, as was her thoughtful way.

Dear Jack,

I feel that to be writing my first fan letter at the grand old age of thirty must be a bit silly, but over the past few months I have come to know and to admire you through your novels. I find great delight in the characters you bring to life for me. It is a curiously new experience to read the words written by a man that I see on the television. In a strange way, I am having a beautiful adventure with you. When I pick up one of your books, I think to myself: I will just sit down with Jack for half an hour. Then, of course, I look forward to our weekly date. I enjoy your programme very much.

Thank you for the many hours of pleasure you have given me. We have a special relationship. If you have time, I would love a signed photo – my children really would think Mum had gone quite mad then!

I only wish that I was clever enough or interesting enough to merit a Jack interview, then we would meet. Your interview concerning the romantic novel interested me. When you asked, 'Is the love affair considered to be the most important thing in an artist's life?' and the reply was, 'Yes, I do', I was captivated.

Love,
Marian Davies

PS I think you should be interviewed about your books – your fans would love to know more about the man behind the characters and how much of you is really in them. Please do think about it. I am willing and able (ha-ha) to give a Marian Davies interview with Jack Kelly – how about it? What a novel idea, the fan interviewing the novelist.

Bye, Marian

I must confess to having been amused by this and rather taken by the openness of her letter. I was flattered to be complimented on my books; it meant even more to me than the programme that I was so proud of. I replied immediately.

Dear Marian Davies,

Thank you very much for your letter. It is fun to make yourself look like a teenager in your children's eyes, so I enclose a public relations photo of me looking rather smug and silly. The fact that you found me through my books is very rewarding because it is a harder medium than television, but your idea to interview me would seem quite outrageous to my production team!

Best wishes,
Yours sincerely,
Jack Kelly

By return of post came...

Dear Jack Kelly,

I am sensible enough to realise that I cannot keep up a correspondence with you but I must thank you for bothering to answer my letter and enclosing a photograph, which, I have to admit, makes you look like an apostle, with your shoulder-length blond hair and new beard. Thank you.

However, please allow me to disagree with you when you say that it's far more difficult to reach people through books than television. I have known you as a personality for years but was not interested in you as a man until I started reading your novels. A novel says so much more about the real person than his television image ever can. Since my first letter, I have read *The Needle*; it is compelling in a very different way from your earlier stories. What excites me, yet disturbs me, is the fact that for the first time

I am able to relate to the novelist who is also a visitor to my home. I have admired the words of many great writers, most of whom are dead. Many have made an impression on me. It is quite a different experience with you being so near and yet so far. I would love to think that one day I will meet you, not because you are famous, but just because I like you. I am a member of a readers' club. Dare I ask if a group of us could have a look around the studio sometime in the future? I should be far too shy to embarrass you with any schoolgirl-like behaviour.

I hope that the lorry drivers' strike won't last too long. We are getting very low on oil for the central heating. I am feeling a bit chilly as I write this because we are only switching the heating on for a few hours a day, so as to conserve the fuel. We need it for hot water too.

Oh, I am rambling on…

Love & best wishes,
Marian Davies

I remember being surprised by her request. It was not usual for the public to visit a recording studio, but I had to admit to being intrigued by her remarks about the novelist as a household visitor. I was reminded of the opinion of a man whose views I valued above all others, Carl Jung. Jung's teaching on the anima and the animus was what my work of late was based on. I had studied his theory on the woman within the male psyche from my own point of view. The man within the woman's psyche I had not explored, but after being approached by this woman from the audience, my pursuit of understanding the human condition became even more interesting.

So, with Jung's thoughts in mind, I pondered on her request for a month or two before answering her letter. I'd had many a muse in the past, but not one attracted by my work; I felt interested by this concept.

Dear Marian Davies,

Thank you for your letter. If you would really like to join us one Monday to look around the studio, I suggest that you contact Bill Bruce – he organises these things. He will do all he can to help you if you mention that I told you to get in touch with him. I assure you that I will make every effort to meet you. I certainly hope that you did get a delivery of oil before your tank was completely empty. There have been too many strikes since the beginning of the year and the rail workers' 24-hour strike meant that we had to cancel a couple of interviews. There is always a knock-on effect to such action. It's not great to see Britain in a state of industrial unrest, with tens of thousands of workers feeling, what has become known as, the winter of discontent.

Best wishes,
Yours sincerely,
Jack Kelly

Dear Jack Kelly,

As per your letter, I contacted Bill Bruce, as you suggested, over a month ago, but I haven't heard from him as yet. I have only recently found out that your current affairs programme is on the radio. I must tell you that my sister-in-law is only just recovering from standing for selection to become a candidate, as a Member of Parliament, for the Labour Party in last year's General Election. She has been treated dreadfully, by groups of both men and women running the local machine on behalf of the national party. She tells me that the process is totally undemocratic and poisonous, allowing only tribal cronies any chance of getting selected. They allow little cliques to manipulate and bully members into voting for who they have already decided should stand. Not for the greater good, but for the good of following the status quo and to keep themselves in power. Nicknamed the 'status crows' by Melanie! Apparently, local councils are mostly run by self-interested psychopaths or egos, who gain fulfilment by making decisions on behalf of the apathetic public. I mention this as I know that you are a champion for the underdog, whichever party.

Melanie says that maybe Margaret Thatcher achieved her wish to become Prime Minister because she had already been propelled into being leader of the Conservative Party by their bully boys. All the parties are the same when it comes to bullying. She is lucky to come along at the time when it is perceived politically correct to make way for a woman. She appears to be her own woman and not to be messed with, but even she must have been anointed by her tribe, before the public had any say in the matter. Now that I have seen what my husband's sister has been through, I realise that the system is flawed and everything fixed. Robert (my husband) tells me it is better than most countries though, and that I ought to remember that. But local councils are run by activists who bring in friends they know will scratch their backs and do as they are told. It makes me so angry when I can see an honest, committed young woman like Melanie trampled on just to perpetuate the mafia-like group in the Town Hall. I am not a party person and after this I never will be. I did campaign for my sister-in-law and enjoyed chatting to people on their doorsteps, but I feel aggrieved for having been taken for a ride in believing that it is an honest and fair system.

Her main objective was to campaign against the probable sell-off of the council houses if Margaret Thatcher were to win the election. She feels that once they are sold, the housing problem will just get worse, with not enough affordable housing available for those who need it. Melanie is not a raving leftie, but a woman who would put her head above the parapet for the sake of others. That's why Labour don't want her. She is an ideas woman and that spells trouble in their eyes. Oh gosh, I seem to be rambling again – sorry! When writing to you, I seem to be able to think of what I feel.

Back to you though, I have just been under the spell of *The Golden Chain*. Both the main characters came very much alive for me. How sad beauty and truth can be. Your latest novel, *Season's Greetings*, has not yet reached our local bookshop, so I look forward to it arriving sometime this summer. They have promised to order it. With so many of your stories in my head, I think of you as a dear friend.

Love & best wishes,
Marian Davies

I was glad that *The Golden Chain* had moved her; it was written as an attempt to psychoanalyse myself after the breakup with my first wife and a hasty remarriage. *Season's Greetings* was describing the negative anima, blaming the mother for having a negative influence. It expressed irritable, depressed moods, uncertainty and insecurity, and was touchy throughout. The whole of my real life at that period seemed to take on a sad and oppressive aspect. I realised that I was just playing a role expected of me, not one I wanted. Writing the book helped me to face the truth.

Time was passing and a meeting with Marian had not been arranged. Looking into the situation, I discovered why, so I instructed my secretary to telephone Mrs Davies to explain that Bill Bruce had been off sick for a couple of months. I asked her to apologise for the delay and to arrange a suitable date before the end of the season. It was agreed that just one friend would accompany Marian before we shut up shop for the summer. As I listened in on the extension ,she sounded pleasantly surprised to hear from us. Her voice was warm and friendly. I liked the sound of her.

A few days before her arrival, I must have felt apprehensive. After all, inviting a complete stranger who might not even look very attractive was unusual. I decided safety in numbers and invited an old school friend who had expressed a desire to take a look around, too. It would also stop any unnecessary gossip.

MARIAN

If I go back to the beginning, it might make some sort of sense. It was Christmas, at the start of the eighties. I went to the library before the celebrations began and picked up two books for the holidays. One was *The Needle* and the other was *Birth Place*, both were by Jack Kelly. I must have been vaguely aware of his name to have decided to pick them off the shelf. After the festivities, between Christmas and New Year, I found it relaxing reading them. As a family we enjoyed the school holidays, happy in the security of our home. We were comfortable and we were happy.

A few weeks into the new year I noticed that *The Times* recommended viewers watch a newish programme called *The Show of Shows* and that Jack Kelly was doing a pretty good job as the editor and the presenter. It was to give a platform to artists from across the spectrum and promised to be both informative and entertaining. I was interested by this and settled down to watch.

My young family were asleep in bed and my husband

was on call at the hospital. I was alone and peaceful, and curious to see the man who had written the two very different books I had just enjoyed. I can see the recording clearly in my mind's eye even now. Jack was interviewing a writer about her novels and in particular her latest one about a successful man who risked everything he had achieved for love. As they ended their conversation, I heard Jack ask, 'Do you think that the love affair is the most important thing in life?' 'Oh, yes, I do,' came the reply. In that brief moment, I was hooked. When the programme finished, I was quick to put pen to paper.

That first letter was the beginning of what was to be a brainstorming experience for me and a part of my life that was both exciting and extraordinary. I was a participant in an intellectual experiment that I thought was just a friendly exchange of ideas. I honestly believed that I was being tolerated because I was a besotted fan. I had no knowledge about psychology and a writer's mind, or anyone's mind for that matter. It was the start of the eighties and I still had a lot to learn. I did like the idea of a 'romance in the mind' – a phrase that I noticed in one of Jack's books. However, I learnt from his work that what I was seeking was intellectual stimulation and fulfilment for my imagination. As Carl Jung would say, I needed to develop my animus – the man within my psyche.

He must have been curious about my letter, because he replied. I have no idea why I gave the impression that I had read all of his books though, or that I looked forward to his programme when I had never even watched it prior to that. I think it was because his written words spoke directly to me and I felt a bond between us immediately. I felt that I could be open with him for some reason; I suppose because I felt honesty in his writing.

I have since wondered about the boldness in writing to a man that I didn't know, except through his work, and a man that I had no intention of ever letting interfere with my marriage. The only explanation I can find is that of the women who write to men on death row: they allow their imaginations to run riot, knowing that person will never be free or a threat to them. My case was rather different from theirs though, because the man I wrote to was very powerful, not powerless and not awaiting the electric chair or the hangman. But I had assumed that because he was a celebrity, he was out of bounds and no threat to me whatsoever. Why would he be interested in me? I had no idea I played with fire by setting light to Jack Kelly's emotions, and that the imagination is best used in being creative – a lesson I learnt from the Master.

JACK

Rereading her letters caused me to think of what was going on politically at the time. *The Show of Shows* was not the only programme I had hosted; I also chaired a weekly radio programme looking over the week's current affairs. It was surprising to think back to the eighties and to contemplate the consensus-style politics that had been in postwar Britain. The main parties mostly agreed on fundamental issues such as the mixed economy, the role of Trades Unions and the need for an incomes policy. The country had seen previous Governments take care of provision of public services for such things as our much-loved health and education services. Little did we know how soon consensus-style politics would start to disappear!

I saw from my lengthy diary notes that only the year before my TV debut, at the end of March '79, James Callaghan's Labour Party had lost a motion of confidence by one vote, forcing a General Election in the May that year. I had discussed the fact that it was the first time television coverage had dominated the campaign as never before and although Margaret Thatcher blamed Callaghan for the Winter of Discontent, she refused to appear alongside him and David Steel, when invited by the television programme *Tomorrow's World*. My guests pointed out that she was aware that Callaghan was popular with the voters. However, she worked very hard to provide photo opportunities, to be seen with her shopping basket, drinking tea in factories or kissing newborn babies. David Steel was also camera-friendly, but he was accused of using stunts that made him look as though he had a large following of supporters, such as for example, by being photographed in narrow streets. Television was starting to play an important part in the battle to win votes.

I had also noted that I was horrified to hear of the car bomb that killed Airey Neave, who was the Conservative spokesperson for Northern Ireland. The IRA had placed the device under his car in the Common's car park. It was a shocking thing to happen to a good man and one that made me ashamed on behalf of the Irish nation. Being Irish myself, I understood the Irish position, but we, the ordinary people of Ireland, didn't agree with terrorist violence. It was shameful and to bring it to the mainland again was a crime against humanity, no matter what they were trying to achieve politically.

In April 1979, the year before my career as a broadcaster on television took off, the economy shrank by 0.8 per cent due to the 'Winter of Discontent' and we were faced with the possibility of a second recession in four years. Budgets became tight and I was extremely fortunate to be offered the contract as a new face of television. My radio approach had won the listeners' ratings and gave me the opportunity to branch out from current affairs into a very broad spectrum of culture. This meant that I became a workaholic because my passion for current affairs continued and I couldn't give it up. I wore two hats and enjoyed being known in every household, despite my Irish accent – or maybe because of it.

The appointed day arrived; Marian was coming to the studio. I felt a bit excited. It would be interesting to see what sort of woman she was. She had said my words reached her – now I had the chance to see what kind of a woman would write so openly to me. I dressed with care that day, wanting to make a good impression. I have to say I hoped she would not be disappointed.

It was arranged that my guests would be taken to the tiny viewing room just before we went on air. I felt that it was best to meet after rather than before the show. When the recording was over, I stood outside the soundproof booth and caught a glimpse of those inside. I knew which of the two women Marian was immediately – a strange innocence in her look told me it was her. I opened the door, popped my head into the room and, without saying hallo, I asked,

'Will you stay for a drink?'

She replied, 'We'd love to.'

I nodded, saying, 'Wait here, then. I have one or two calls to make. Someone will fetch you to the hospitality room. Don't move, though, or you will never be seen again in this huge maze of a building.'

Later, in the Green Room, I positioned myself between my school friend Mark and the producer, with other members of the crew on either side. My growing celebrity meant that I had a protection team with me when in public. Fans on the street and at book venues did like to get up close and personal at times. Marian and her friend were ushered in by my secretary. We shook hands and I said, formally, 'It is very nice to meet you.'

'Never having been to a studio before, it is very interesting. Thank you for letting us come,' she replied equally formally.

About a dozen of us stood around chatting for an hour or so. In that time, she and I exchanged but a few sentences. She stood opposite in the circle of friendly chatter. I did make one direct remark to her,

'I'm glad you liked the books.'

Without changing her expression, she replied, 'You must forgive my letters for being personal but I felt that I had taken the books over.'

Holding her gaze, I said, 'I have felt that myself about other people's books.'

Her quiet response was, 'I'm sure.'

We both nodded at a shared experience. I felt the need to move away, a shyness befell me, and as I did we caught each other's look. I sat across the room, pretending to listen to the producer, only now and then allowing myself to glance over to her. She seemed unaware of me, intent on conversation with those around her. On reflection, I realise that we didn't flirt. There was a mutual bond between us, though. I felt it. That was why I moved away, best to keep her at a distance and let my fantasy dwell upon her in my creative mind. As people started to make tracks for home, my secretary informed me that Mrs Davies was leaving.

'Are you off?' I asked stupidly.

'Yes. Once again, thank you for letting us come.' She smiled as we shook hands.

'Goodbye.'

That was that. As the room emptied, I was left with Mark and Ron, feeling a little flat. I wanted Mark to feel that he could take his time because he had got a day off work to visit me and seemed to be enjoying himself.

Some thirty minutes later, the door opened and a shy face looked directly at me, walking across the room. Marian held out a copy of my latest book, *Season's Greetings*.

'Did you find us all right?' I asked, surprised that she had found her way back to us as every floor looked the same in the modern concrete building.

'No, I got horribly lost! I almost forgot that I had this in the car, will you sign it?' she asked.

'I could wish it were another,' I moaned.

'They said some rude things about that one, I remember.' Mark volunteered this as he recognised the cover. He and I both nodded in agreement.

'Oh well. It is the latest one,' she insisted.

Reluctantly, I signed and dated a page; she turned to go immediately. Before she reached the door, I asked, 'Do you know where to go?'

'Not really. Is it left and then right, through the swing doors?' she asked as she glanced back over her shoulder.

'Left, then straight ahead to the lifts,' I replied.

Once again we held each other's look, then I turned my head away. When I glanced back, she was gone.

After her visit, I jotted down a few notes in my writer's

notebook. I found it hard to repress thoughts of her. What had happened to me was like a blow to the whole body, as if Marian was a force of nature so strong that every part of me was struck and weakened by it. My first wife had left me to marry a rock star, leaving me feeling empty and, yes, selfish. I now realise that I was just waiting, indeed longing, for the sweet sensation of love. My second marriage was useful but not colourful.

My artistic self responded to the image of Marian and my plan had been to use her in a simple psychological way to further my development as an individual, as well as a creative writer and editor. I was taken unawares and completely shocked by what she awoke in me; it was the most powerful need and lustfulness, and my intuition recognised it even though I tried hard to ignore it. I did fall head over heels in love, not with her but with the thing inside me that so wanted an object on which to place my fancy. I say that now, in hindsight, as I read through her letters, as my memory recalls that brief encounter.

I had many female admirers, some in everyday life and many as fans, but I knew that in this simple encounter I had to turn her head; I had found a fly for a web that I so yearned to weave. It was a sort of madness I had been fighting since my teens. Puberty had left me feeling psychologically disturbed in a strange way. I had felt it as a sort of frenzy that sex in itself was not able to fulfil. The best way to describe it is that I had been bitten by a bee, a bee that I was allergic to and to which my whole body was reacting to. It was as if the sting was infused into my bloodstream and I was helpless against its poison, and the more it hurt, the more I liked it. Marian could be the blossom and I felt that if I was able to buzz around her, it might be possible to make more and more honey. I was used to being the pollen around which my fans hovered at book signings and I received a lot of fan mail about me as a sexy presenter. Now, though, it was very different because I had been stung. I had to find a way to further enslave Marian so as to manipulate her imagination under my control. But I didn't see that I was in danger of falling under her control if our correspondence continued. I hadn't experienced the power of the muse; I had only read about other, older, writers' encounters in that respect. All I knew was that my Arts programme had to become the hive where I hoarded away the honey from the busy worker bees. As she left me on that one and only meeting, I saw that she too felt the bee's sting immediately. My eyes were held as if by a sticky drizzle of syrup to hers and I was aware that they couldn't turn away from her gaze without the deliberate effort of turning my head. It was an alarming experience trying to break the thread, as if a spider, not a bee, had woven us together across the empty space of the room. When she left, I knew I had found that feeling I had longed for and I was aware that something in me changed and I was greedy to feed the hunger I felt deep inside. I had not allowed myself to deliberately captivate a female for the sake of my art before. I had tried to concentrate on my work without pursuing a victim. After we met, my imagination urged me on like a criminal who must break into a person's home, in order to hold them hostage.

Two days later, a thank-you note arrived:

Dear Jack,

Thank you for everything; you remain a romance in my mind.

Marian.

PS 'a romance in the mind' is something that you write of often!

Once again, I consulted Carl Jung. His writing encouraged the following:

'But what does the role of the anima as guide to the inner world mean in practical terms?

This positive function occurs when a man takes seriously the feelings, moods, expectations and fantasies sent by his anima and when he fixes them in some form – for example, in writing, painting, musical composition etc. etc. When he works at this patiently and slowly, other more deeply unconscious material wells up from the depths and connects with the earlier material. After a fantasy has been fixed in some specific form, it must be examined both intellectually and ethically, with an evaluating feeling reaction. And it is essential to regard it as being absolutely real; there must be no lurking doubt that this is only a fantasy. If this is practised with devotion over a long period, the process of individuation gradually becomes the single reality and can unfold in its true form. Only the painful (but essentially simple) decision to take one's fantasies and feelings seriously can, at this stage, prevent a complete stagnation of the inner process of individuation, because only in this way can a man discover what this figure means as an inner reality. Thus, the anima becomes again what she originally was –'the woman within', she conveys vital messages to the Self.'

I had read all that before; it now helped me to decide to use the idea of this strangely attractive woman to help me live out my fantasies in a creative way and to develop the Self. What great timing for this psychological experiment, when I was free to use material on the programme and play God in my editing room. I felt that I could promote the work of others while fulfilling myself, too.

My own writing was but one way to express myself. I thought long and hard on the exciting possibility of editing the spoken word of other artists in order to get my own thoughts across the airwaves to the attentive ears of Marian. I felt like a schoolboy hiding away in the darkened room with a box of tricks, so explosive that I could well have been working on an undercover secret mission. The works would disguise my hidden meaning and be coded so that the world would not decipher it. And I would do it in front of the nation as I informed and entertained them. The power of the editor was like an aphrodisiac. The dawning of Facebook and Twitter was still many decades away and hosting a user-friendly Arts programme was very much a novelty. It excited me to use the programme as a vehicle to communicate. To use the television screen as a monitor was ahead of its time, making use of the electronic equipment of the day to reach out, sending my message, with its hidden meaning, loud and clear. It would be public yet private.

I had to think of how to coach Marian's ear to pick up

on my intent. I was about to take a summer break when, to my delight, I received the following letter from her.

Dear Jack,

I want to write to you again before you leave London for the summer in Ireland. I could cry when I think that I had the chance to talk to you and did no more than make polite conversation. What I really wanted to say when I met you was that I read your books greedily one after the other and now I feel hungry for your words. I felt so very involved with you through your stories that now I miss you. Please do not think of me as a frustrated suburban housewife. Through your writing you fulfilled a need in me, as though you were writing just for me. I look forward to the return of the programme later in the year – what a long gap. I know that I am daft to fall in love with a man through his books, but maybe it happens quite often to your readers and you are used to it. Jack, I don't expect you to answer this letter; you have been more than kind already. It helps me to put pen to paper and confess; it must be my Catholic upbringing!

Love to you,
Marian

I instructed my secretary that we were not answering this and she duly noted this across the top of the letter.

I decided that I would spend the summer writing a new book and psychoanalyse my inner world. Ever since writing *The Needle*, I had turned to Jung, Freud, Proust and André Gide for guidance. Their thoughts and experiences helped me through a very difficult period of my life. *The Needle* was the first time that I had used the dream-world symbols in order to express how I was feeling. That summer, I wrote *Birth Place*, the story of different women, thus meaning that I was hopeful of new possibilities. It expressed the need for a spiritual union, the desire to be wooed and the fear of disappointment. I felt an excitement when writing this, as I was sure that Marian would read it, and I could put a face before me when alone with my thoughts. I was speaking directly to myself when using the symbolic images, though. I didn't want Marian or anybody knowing what I was really doing. It pleased me to have a code in which to hide, while at the same time helping me to understand myself. I knew I was a complex personality with the need to be secretive. I suppose it gave me a sense of security to write one thing but to mean another. It was a double-edged sword, in order to defend myself against the harsh realities of life. I could express my desires and human condition without hurting anybody. The respectable life was endurable with this safety valve as a release. My imagination would save me from myself and was already earning me a very good living.

MARIAN

The day I went to the studio, I felt a bit silly, because I didn't really know what to expect. I had never been a groupie following the Beatles or the Rolling Stones and I only ever saw Elvis or Cliff Richard in films. So the idea of going to see a novelist, who appeared on the television, record one of his programmes was quite out of character for me. My family didn't seem to think it strange; I think they thought it was just a nice thing to do.

I remember wearing a red skirt and a matching blouse, with a black belt and black court shoes. I felt that I looked nice and I know that I always looked respectable, never sexy, unless feminine would be judged that way. I washed and blow-dried my hair, and was glad that it went well, and after I'd put on some foundation, lipstick and eye shadow, I double-checked myself in the mirror and caught a smile flicker across my face. I think I felt grown up getting ready to go on an outing that didn't include my husband, three sons or my daughter. I hadn't done much, if anything, on my own since leaving my job to have our first baby. It felt nice, not exciting but pleasant. I was doing something just for me. I rang my friend to let her know that I was about to pick her up, but her line was engaged. It seems strange now to think that the landline was the only means of contacting someone then, but it was. I waited for the line to be free – no chance then of a quick text message to say that I was on my way.

Helen looked pretty as she got into the car and we giggled about the chance of meeting the famous Jack Kelly, feeling, I think, like naughty teenagers who had been given permission to go out on the spree for a few hours. The traffic was not too busy around that time of the day so we arrived in the car park within about half an hour of leaving home, which meant that we had an hour to wait before our appointed time of arrival. I always drove into London in those days.

'I wonder what he will be like,' Helen mused.

'I can't imagine. I am beginning to wonder what we are doing here,' I answered as we laughed.

'Have we gone mad?' I suggested. Helen bit on her lip, then said, 'I think perhaps we have!'

We continued like that for the rest of the time, urging each other to turn tail and run for home.

'I wonder why he agreed for us to come?' Helen asked.

'Maybe it's normal for fans to write in and make such a request,' I replied. 'I was surprised that he even engaged in correspondence with me and bothered to send a signed photograph. I suppose it must happen all of the time.'

'Yes, or maybe his agent does all that just to keep the ratings for the programme up,' Helen offered.

'Oh, don't say that. I felt that it was him responding to me. That would be awful and embarrassing.'

I pulled a face, imagining Jack being forced into meeting a couple of silly women whom he hadn't really wanted to meet in the first place.

'Ah well, the country has recently voted in a woman to be Prime Minster for the first time in our history, so I suppose us women shouldn't be shy about popping into a studio for a couple of hours!' Helen winked at me as she said this.

She was right, the Conservative Party had been voted in and Margaret Thatcher had become PM; maybe this fact had something to do with this visit. Had it started me thinking outside the box without even realising it? I had tried not to take much notice because I was still smarting over my sister-in-law Melanie's experience with politics. But it had been exciting to see a woman achieve the highest political position in the land, surprising too because when she had been a minister she had become known as 'Maggie Thatcher, the milk snatcher.' She had taken away the daily bottle of milk from schoolchildren and within a few months of her reign, milk was to increase by more than 10 per cent to 15p per pint. As a Mum, I had noticed that.

Robert had long debates in our home with his sister and his parents. Much of what they said went over my head. Looking after the children took up most of my time and I was ready to unwind with my feet up by the time such conversations got going. The Tory Manifesto had promised to control inflation and to keep the unions in check. There had been fears of a deeper recession with the previous

Callaghan government and people were afraid that the unions had become too powerful. Margaret's case might have been helped too by the ex-Labour Prime Minister, Harold Wilson, declaring that his wife Mary might vote Tory just to support a woman into office. Also, the Tory advertising campaign, directed by Saatchi & Saatchi, claimed that 'Labour isn't working.' So Britain's first woman Prime Minister was voted in with a safe working majority; the swing, to the Conservatives, of 5.2 per cent gave them the largest majority since 1945.

I made the tea and provided the biscuits while this grown-up talk went on. I was glad to have helped our eldest with his homework and have time to myself before bed, but even so the message got through to me, drip by drip.

Helen and I chatted about this as we sat in the car. Neither of us were activists for any party, but with our families growing up we were starting to take notice of the current situation in Britain. The evening television news was full of the change afoot and we were vaguely aware of the unrest that had been bubbling up over the past decade. There was no such thing as rolling news, of course, so as suburban housewives we were not well informed. Helen and I were both fortunate in that our husbands had good careers and we were provided for. Our mission in life was to run the home and look after the children. We both made that our full-time job. Remember, I am talking about the very early eighties.

The hour soon passed and we made our way to the reception at the front desk. I announced that we had come at the invitation of Jack Kelly, to see the recording of *The Show of Shows.* The receptionist directed us to sit down and told us that Jack's secretary would soon be along to fetch us. Helen and I took a seat in the foyer, glancing up each time a young woman passed us, in anticipation of being collected. Just before three o'clock, we found ourselves on the basement floor of the building, inside a viewing booth, waiting for the programme to begin. A man was already sitting in there, who was introduced to us as Jack's old school friend, Mark. We three sat in the dark, looking through the glass panel at the well-lit studio, facing an empty desk and chair, while the cameramen and the production team tested the equipment.

Then, Jack walked through the door to take a seat behind the desk. He looked well groomed in his tailored suit and long, fashionable hairstyle. He didn't acknowledge us, but after a cue he started to introduce an already-recorded act, which was screened onto a monitor in front of us. I think we were expecting it all to be live; instead, it was pre-recorded and rolled out and stopped at the appropriate times to allow Jack to talk between the recordings. I was fascinated by the process, so much so that I can't even remember who was actually featured that day. I was just impressed by the proceedings. Within the hour, it was all done and dusted and Jack made funny faces and cracked a few jokes that we couldn't hear before he left the studio floor.

The door to the viewing booth opened as he popped his head in and, without asking who we were, looked straight at me. 'Will you stay for a drink?' he asked.

'We would love to.' I was quick to answer.

He looked very serious as he stressed that we were to stay where we were until someone came to collect us, to take us to the Green Room. He made a point of saying that we would never be seen again in the tall building if we ventured out on our own – he was convinced that we would get lost. He had a few calls to make apparently, before he would be free to join us.

Mark chatted to us and he told us that he had used the new Jubilee line to get to the studio – it had opened that month. He explained that he was nervous about the future because of the proposal to sell off the Government's stake in British Petroleum and that nationalised industries were under threat and a lot of jobs would go. I was able to say that my eldest boy was pleased because he had secured a summer job at the newly opened Thorpe Park in Surrey; it was to become the third most popular theme park in the UK.

Suddenly we were stepping out of the lift on the tenth floor, behind Jack's secretary. She showed us into a rather boring-looking modern room, which was used for hospitality after recordings of all the different television programmes made there had taken place. It was a bit disappointing being in the functional room on top of the entire box-like building and surprising to me that so many lively, interesting, energetic programmes were housed in such a concrete slab of architecture. I suppose I felt that art ought to be conceived in beautiful places, just as I felt that mass ought to be said in beautiful churches. I was a lover of meaningful structure, not just the soft centre of things.

We walked across the room to where Jack was standing in the middle of some of the team. As we approached, his secretary introduced Helen and myself to him. We shook hands and I was struck by his long fingers with large manicured nails. They weren't like any hands I had seen before; they seemed unusual to me. He was very self-contained as he said how nice it was to meet us. I remember saying something about how interesting it was to be there as it was all quite new to us, to watch a recording. I think I mentioned that I loved his books and that I'd felt taken over by them, and as I said that a glance between us seemed to say more than words. He nodded and said that he knew what I meant, because other writers had affected him in that way.

A glass of wine was offered to us and we turned away from Jack's group, engaging in conversation with a couple of members of the team. It was all very friendly, concerning different aspects of the programme and the artists that had appeared on it. They even asked us for ideas about who to include in coming seasons. The time passed in a flash and I became aware that people were starting to go, so I felt that we ought to take our leave and not outstay our welcome.

Jack's secretary took us back over to him, explaining that we were about to go home.

Looking up, he said rather feebly, 'Are you off?'

He stood up and once again we shook hands and I thanked him for letting us join him. He smiled his boyish smile and we turned on our heels and left the room, being shown to the lift by his ever-patient PA. It had been very nice, but it all felt a bit flat when Helen and I got back to the car.

'It was very nice and so was he.' Helen grinned at me.

'Yes, but it all seemed to go so fast. We hardly spoke to him,' I responded, spotting a copy of his latest book on the back seat.

'Oh, Helen, look, I forgot to take this in to get it signed. Wait here, I won't be long. I have to go back, I really do. That's what I came for!'

I slammed the car door shut before she had time to answer, almost running in my haste to catch him before he too left the building. I rushed past reception without a word to them, making straight for the lift. I wasn't even sure which floor we had been on, but my hunch proved to be right and somehow I made it to the Green Room unguided. When I pushed the door open and held out his book as I approached him, I said earnestly, 'Look, I almost forgot I had this with me. Please will you sign it?'

He was sitting with Mark and one other man and he pulled a face as he caught sight of the sleeve. 'I could wish it were another,' he confessed as Mark made some rude remark about the critics.

'Oh, well. It's your latest, so that's all right,' I encouraged.

He signed his autograph and the minute he handed the book back to me, I turned to go.

'Thank you,' I said, glancing over my shoulder.

In that split second, we held each other's gaze for the second time; a sense of knowing was between us, but I didn't know what of.

'Do you know where to go?' he asked.

'Not really is it left and then right, through the swing door? I replied, glancing back again.

'Left, then straight on,' he replied.

Instead of turning his eyes from me, he lifted his chin, moving his whole face away as if he couldn't move just his eyes. The unusual movement made me feel he was sorry to see me go. It will seem fanciful to recall it now, but I was aware of rays of light streaming from his eyes as he looked away, as if electric beams were pulsing from them. I couldn't understand it then and I can't explain it now, but it happened. There was a connection that I had never experienced before.

After that, I wrote expressing regret at not having taken the chance to really speak to him and it was at least six months before we were in contact again. Looking back, I can see that he had devised a plan to entrap me in his forthcoming programmes, but at the time I hadn't the slightest idea of that. I conducted myself like a devoted fan, enjoying nothing more than fan mail to my favourite writer, not knowing his scheming plot to capture my imagination so as to groom me to listen to his every word. Others may say that he was trying to inspire me, but it was much more than that.

JACK

My childhood home in Ireland was the sanctuary that I retreated to whenever I needed to be alone with myself, in order to write. It was my spiritual home and vital to my creative world within. After a while though, it was always good to get back to London for the new season. The Irish countryside was great, but London was the hub of the universe for a programme-maker like me. The planning for each year took place well in advance, so my control over Marian would take some time to implement. I had to be patient and follow a gently, gently approach so as not to arouse suspicion from the team or the viewing public. I was sure that once on air I would hear from Marian; that was the all-important thing, keeping her out there.

While I was in Ireland, during August, the tragic assassination of the Duke of Edinburgh's uncle, Lord Mountbatten of Burma, and his nephew and boat boy, by a Provisional IRA bomb took place. Like me, they were on holiday in the Republic of Ireland. It was made even sadder because Mountbatten loved Ireland and its people. Before the month was out, two men were arrested in Dublin and charged with the murders. I was called upon by the BBC to host a radio special on the event during the same month that eighteen British soldiers were also killed in Northern Ireland by IRA bombs. It was a terribly sad time, when the IRA terrorists were very active. Most of the Nationalist population were as horrified as I was and I wanted the British people to understand the Irish situation and to realise that England and Ireland had a very bad history that needed to be put to rest, once and for all. We needed a non-violent, political solution, something that seemed impossible at the time.

In September I returned to the UK, glad to get back to kick-start the editing of the forthcoming programmes. My good friend Nadia was over from India and popped into the studio. She mentioned that Briton Martin Webster was found guilty of inciting racial hatred; he was from the far right politically at the time. She was on a two-year assignment to London for her local rag because the general unrest within the UK was starting to receive worldwide attention. She had studied in Dublin and was concerned by the problems that were evolving. It was good to see her again as we'd been to debates together, and we shared the love of the British but we also understood the trouble that nationalism could cause.

Plans were afoot, by the production team, for Godfrey Hounsfield and Allan McLeod Cormack to be portrayed during our new season. They had won jointly the Nobel Prize in Physiology or Medicine for 'The Development of Computer Assisted Tomography'. It wasn't a subject we would normally cover, but it seemed of interest to some of our viewers at that time. Before I departed to interview them my secretary gave me the currency for my trip to Scandinavia. I was interested to see from my notes that she had ordered more than usual because all remaining foreign exchange controls had just been abolished in the UK. It was significant enough for me to note; before then, only a very limited amount of cash had been allowed out of the country as foreign currency. Prior to this banks had to mark and date the amount in the passport, too.

A couple of weeks into the programme, my patience paid off!

Dear Jack,

It is nice to see you back on the air and I have enjoyed the first three weeks. I'm about to take a short course on how to use a computer. The thought of it interests me but I have no idea what to expect. When I was with you, a member of your team asked for possible features to cover and as I am lost in the beautiful English of D. H. Lawrence's *The Rainbow*, I thought how interesting it would be if you were to explain Lawrence the man. Richard Aldington's introduction, at the front of the book, is all I know of his life, but there must be lots to tell concerning the persecution that was inflicted on him. Somerset Maugham, another of my favourite writers, would also make an interesting subject. And what about the new pop group calling themselves Spandau Ballet, and Elton John who was the first musician to visit the Soviet Union from the West in May this year? The list is never-ending of the artists from A–Z you could interview. So exciting! How nice it would be if my favourite living writer would sum some of them up. It's just a thought.

Best wishes,
Marian Davies

PS It is good that *The Times* is being published again after nearly a year, so the dispute between management and unions, over staffing levels and new technology, must be over. I might find you in it any day now! M

I waited about five weeks, until just before Christmas, to reply. My plan was that she would be eager to receive word from me and that her anticipation would mean she would follow the programmes intently. I hoped she would be waiting for a sign that I was still thinking of her and that she would then look forward to the next series that I was fine-tuning.

Dear Marian Davies,

Thank you for your letter and kind comments. It is good to receive your ideas.

Best wishes for Christmas and the New Year.
Yours sincerely,
Jack

I wanted to hold her attention, but would keep my replies formal – let my art speak for itself in good time. The programmes continued and I heard no more from her until near the end of February when she just sent a card congratulating me on the compliments that I was receiving and on a book award I'd won. Then, my latest book was published; I knew that she had a hard copy of my previous novel and I hoped that she would purchase one this time. The paperback would not be out for at least another year. I waited…

Dear Jack,

Once again I am sad because I have finished another of your books, *Birth Place*. It gave me much pleasure, thank you. I am amazed by the way you understand people, young and old, the good and the not so good. I think that I would be afraid of you, that you would know my next move, before I did.

Visiting the West End last week, I was surprised to realise that one whole year has passed since my enjoyable visit to the studio. How quickly time goes by. I meant to mention earlier that the only item that did not ring true in *Birth Place* was the fabric of Helena's underwear; satin is not often seen these days in everyday underwear. Man-made fabric is a lot cheaper. No charge for that piece of useless information!

Please let me know when to look forward to your next publication.

Love from,
Marian Davies

I wanted to show her that I was pleased to get this friendly little note, so I replied by using her first name, even though she still signed her surname. I wanted to gain her confidence because I had an idea for the next season. So, I instructed my secretary to use my personal letter heading, which included my direct line and number.

Dear Marian,

I am genuinely delighted that you enjoyed *Birth Place*. It's lovely of you to comment on my books and to give me little tips. The fact that you remember your visit to see me is very pleasing.

Best wishes,
Yours sincerely,
Jack Kelly

It pleased me to send this to reach her on the anniversary of when we'd met. I had noted the precise day. I was biding my time behind the show, careful not to alert the team to my hidden meanings. Playing with visual clips and edited words, so as to send gentle suggestions to the unsuspecting Marian. I was like the hypnotist who knows that his participant is in the real world while their subconscious is spoken to directly. I needed to perfect my skill patiently, without rushing, until I knew for sure that Marian was in the willing state of trance. She had to want a hidden message for it to work and work I was determined that it would, given time. A year had come and gone since we had met and I had already planted the idea in her head that anything can be whatever we want it to be, if we use our imagination.

During the summer, once again, I embedded myself in Ireland. Our old castle had once belonged to an English landowner whose family had been given a title and land for favours to Queen Elizabeth I of England. The family moved out of Ireland back in the 1960s, leaving the cold building to fall into rack and ruin. It suited my wife Pauline and me when I bought it after deciding on some renovation work. We realised that I would have plenty of space to write in one of the old towers and she and the children could relax in the rambling old place during the holidays each year. I flew backwards and forwards to London, to arrange interviews that were to be shown once the autumn series started. I had plenty of time to plan my path into Marian's mind as I made notes on how I would edit the forthcoming programmes so as to continue to tickle her ear.

When I returned to the office after the summer break, a card was on my desk. On the front was a printed commercial verse.

RECEIVING YOUR LETTER GAVE ME MUCH PLEASURE,
ALTHOUGH YOU NEVER SEE ME AND
ALTHOUGH I SELDOM WRITE TO YOU
I HAVE WRITTEN A THOUSAND LETTERS
TO YOU IN MY THOUGHTS.

Inside, she had written…

'I could not resist!'
Bye, Marian

PS Keep safe. The BBC coverage of the SAS
storming the Iranian Embassy in Knightsbridge was
scary. Imagine, they killed five of the six terrorists
and freed all the hostages. It was like watching a
Bond movie! I had never seen live news coverage
like that before.

There was no more communication until late September.
In the meantime, I was busy with the next season's agenda.
I intended, or should I say hoped, to really make her use
her imagination. It is every artist's dream to be able to prove
his/her worth by inspiring another to become creative – a
'brainchild', you might say. If I could get her to follow my
train of thought, who knew what she might be capable of?
I had to try.

MARIAN

Unrest was very real in the UK and yet I continued to live in the comfort of a loving marriage and a happy family. Looking back, I feel very self-indulgent for the experience that I paved for myself; along the path, the yellow brick road was leading to the wizard. I was unsuspecting that he was, in fact, a wizard of the imagination, who had every intention of stirring up his cauldron of spells in his cutting room.

When I think of the violent protests on the streets of this country during that time, I am filled with bewilderment that I didn't take more notice of what was going on in society. Melanie was constantly telling me about the rioting that was happening throughout the country and she and Robert were very animated during 1981 when the whole of England seemed besieged with riots in cities from the North to the South. It is only as I look back that I wonder whether I was deliberately ignoring the hardship of the unemployed and the racial prejudices that were happening, so as to keep us secure as a family unit. Or was I so selfish that it didn't matter to me? In my world, I only ever knew about the situation if I bothered to tune in to the evening news coverage or picked up an occasional newspaper, or listened to Robert and his sister talking it over. I was shocked by people having to live in fear of the bombs from the IRA, and hunger strikers dying for a cause they believed in. But I wasn't affected by the horror of it all and I was cushioned from the public spending cuts and racial hatred, not to mention the workers fighting to keep their jobs. I lived in a local land of plenty; I wanted for nothing in my make-believe world, where I was corresponding with Jack. I seem to have been a Stepford wife and mother in reality. How did I do it. How was I so sheltered? I know that I had the security of Robert to thank for that and my parents, who wrapped me in cotton wool and encouraged me to believe in my safe world. My mother always said that I was born lucky and that it was better to be born lucky than rich.

My family was my whole life. I was not seeking to change my life, but to add colour to the life I already had. I didn't even know that was what I was doing, but events will prove this to be true. I was innocent and naïve, from a world unrecognisable now. Convent-educated, when nuns were nuns and girls like me were protected from the harsh reality of life. I lived in a fairy-tale bubble and even though I was married with four children, I had no idea of the dark side of most people's lives. Being an only child, privately educated and brought up on Hollywood movies in the fifties, I didn't realise that I was taking on one of the intellects of my time. Jack Kelly, I was told, was a brilliant man and I treated him as such until I found out he had feet of clay. I hadn't realised

I was being daring. I acted in a childlike way, which felt so acceptable, having no idea of the consequences of my actions at all. I had no way of knowing what would happen.

I did know that I was being drawn more and more to him and I marvelled in the fact he seemed to like hearing from me. My family knew that I was sending the odd fan mail, but I didn't even mention Jack to Helen again. He was not in my day-to-day life. I zoned in on the evenings when he was on air and I got lost in the subjects that he was interviewing or talking about, and I did feel very close to him when reading his written word. I must admit I did wonder that he bothered with me, but I assumed that many other fans were getting his attention, too. He had a high profile when television was well and truly in its heyday, and the nation was becoming more and more aware of him as a celebrity. I liked the fact that he was on a pedestal, safely out of reach and no danger to my marriage. I felt safe and just a little bit privileged.

I couldn't resist sending the card that seemed to say it all, but then I went quiet for three or four months after sending it. The tabloids had run an article on him at the start of the summer and his wife had given a few statements about the family home being in Ireland each summer. I found myself thinking of his fiction and that close feeling that he had of the land and the people of Ireland, and I understood that it was his Irish roots and love of the country that I related to in his books.

The fact that he was born in Ireland and knew of the things I treasured from my childhood, and that his family were from the same sort of farming stock as mine, had everything to do with why I was so drawn to his writing. My father had filled my imagination, as a little girl, with his stories from his homeland. Having been born in London and having a parent from another country, I found it very intoxicating and I delighted in tales about daddy's childhood and nonsenses such as the fact that the sun always shone in Ireland. All I knew of then was the hustle and the bustle of city life and I thrilled at the sound of his Irish accent while sitting on his big lap, as he whispered sweet nothings into my ear. The contrast between his childhood and mine in London meant that he need make nothing up and he instilled in me a fondness of his land that I will wear in my heart for ever.

Arles, where my father was born, is about five miles outside the town of Carlow. It is on high ground, built on a ridge. It is not a pretty village, but it does overlook very pretty farmland and the river Barrow runs beneath it, in the meadows below. The river acts as a boundary between County Carlow and County Laois. Although Arles is not within the county of Carlow, Carlow was the town that serviced it. Today, in a car, the town of Portlaoise is easily accessible, being only fourteen miles away. Back then, it made sense to trade in and with the local town. In my father's day, the railway was vital to the prosperity of the town and played an exciting part in country people's lives. He told me that the daily newspapers arrived from Dublin on the 8am train and that he could recall there had been trains going up and down to the capital at 8, 10 and 12 in the mornings and later at 3, 6 and 9pm. He said that it was great on a summer's evening to walk behind the church and wait with a group of boys for the train, with its trail of smoke waving through the countryside, to appear in the valley below. He was able to see the train as it left Maganey station heading towards Carlow, bringing home day-trippers from Dublin, after a football match or a demonstration. Standing there amongst the gravestones, he said, was a wonderful experience that might not be imagined today. His mind was entertained as if watching a film, with the landscape in the distance below and the Wicklow Mountains in the background. The seasons appeared as if in a film with the weather setting the scene.

I could tell that was the spot that inspired his imagination, causing him to eventually leave home for a foreign shore, the promise of adventure, in a world waiting to swallow him up in its vastness. He had no means of seeing the world beyond that point. Television had not been invented and the only radio was owned by Father Lawlor, the parish priest. Father Lawlor had cut down the branches from a tree and fixed a wire to run from it to the window of the presbytery, thus making an aerial for his battery-operated transmitter.

'That was the first time I heard English accents from across the sea!' he told me.

He had often mentioned little things like that; he was pleased that Ireland had become prosperous, but he liked to remember the world that he had known when life was simple and the seasons mattered. It was a time when people cared about each other, and manners and respect were everything. He had lived all his life as a gentle man, despite the bursts of temper he had never quite learned to control.

He had believed that manners maketh man (and woman, in particular). He was a good father and I had grown up always wanting to please him.

We had spent many magical summer holidays in Ireland during the 1950s. The Ireland of that era had not changed much from the way it had been at the beginning of the twentieth century. My relatives, all prosperous farmers, still didn't have electricity or running water. Many of the benefits of the twentieth century had not reached out much further than Dublin. As a Londoner, I found all of that exciting. I felt as if I were in a novel and that life had stood still especially for me to experience it. To me, the country that my father had come from was full of mystery and romance.

He had been very proud of the fact that his was one of the leading families in the fertile farming land just south of Dublin. He was shy when telling me this though, as if he had no right to put labels on the likes of farm labourers or the postman. He would say there was the priest, the teacher, the wealthy farm owners and the doctor, who was the only car owner; the rest were working class. We must remember that in 1911, when he was born, village life was very class-conscious and money and land were deferred to. Neither the First World War nor the Russian Revolution had started then, both of which brought about huge changes in society. He came from a place called Arles and his words painted as colourful a picture in my head as Vincent Van Gough did with his paints; he too lived in a town of the same spelling, in the South of France.

I have photographs that are discoloured with age and memories of his stories come flooding back to me.

The house in which he had been born stood opposite the church, across the road that ran through the village. He explained that standing in the front parlour, he would look across at the church. A small window framed it, as if on a television screen, although, of course, he had never heard of such an invention then. I could tell that all of life's drama was seen through that window, as if in a snapshot. The theatre of the Roman Catholic Church, with all of its rich rituals, played a huge part in his young life. Living so close, he and his brothers were called upon by the parish priest to serve on the altar, not just for the Sunday Mass or holy days of obligation, but for christenings, weddings and funerals. He would have stood there in his altar boy vestments, with his back to the congregation and his gaze on the crucifix ahead. The sound of the Latin would have filled his ears, mesmerising him with its strange beauty, as his mind wandered out into the fields beyond. A game of football would await him and a laugh with his friends after, away from the solemn service of the Mass. He liked it best when he attended at a christening or a wedding because then he earned a sixpence, which went a long way then, enabling him to buy a penny whistle or save towards a new piece for his beloved Meccano set.

Even if he was at school, he would be called out to serve, whether it was to help to baptise them, marry them or to bury them; he knew everyone from miles around. The whole congregation would have known Mick Clancy and he would have known them. But I had been surprised to learn from him that daily attendance at Mass had been very low, with only his mother and Mrs Shannon participating. I had supposed that rural Ireland back then would have been more devout on a daily basis. Sundays and holy days though the church was packed.

He saw all of life on that stage, from the cradle to the grave. When he was not in it, he observed it; with its tall steeple, grey stone and wooden door, it shaped the man that he was to become. He didn't have electricity to light his way or to entertain him, but he had the beauty of the Latin and the pain of Our Lord to influence his thinking. The joy of life and the sorrow of death weaved their way into his imagination and made him both sensitive and tough. He could have had little idea of the world beyond his kin until he became a man and went across the sea to England.

I had forgotten much about that part of his life until I began to read Jack's books, only then did I start to understand the significance of that world. Jack's characters spoke to me in a way that my father had. Jack wrote about his family and that awoke memories of my own. I felt a kindred spirit in Jack; he had helped to rekindle the love that was bred in me for Ireland and I felt at ease and comforted by it. My father had woven a rich tapestry with his tales of days gone by, just as Jack did in his novels, and I came to understand more about my father than I could ever have hoped by merely dwelling on him.

During my correspondence with Jack, I had no idea where he and his family had their family retreat, but I imagined it would be within easy reach of an airport. It was reported that he liked having a home in Ireland because it was so quick to pop across to London and back again, after the working day.

JACK

As I said, it was late September before I heard from her again.

Dear Jack,

Hallo, I was pleased to read your article in the *Sunday Times* a few weeks ago and again yesterday in the *Telegraph*. How do you find the time? I am amazed. Also, I enjoyed hearing you on *Any Questions* earlier in the year and now and again on other radio shows. However, please get on with your next novel. I am anxious. I look to you as my intellectual pin-up to enrich my life through your books. A friend of mine is about to write to you regarding her first book, which has just been published in America. It is a pleasing little book of human interest and she would love advice regarding publication in England.

You must forgive me for writing from time to

time, but you worked your way into my mind and seem quite happy to stay there. I am a sensible wife and Mum who just enjoys this little romance of the mind. I look forward to hearing from you even though I realise what a busy man you are.

Bye, love from,
Marian Davies

I was so glad that she was back in contact that I replied by return of post.

Dear Marian,

Thank you very much for writing; I enjoy getting your letters. It is very rewarding having such a devoted fan. I am giving myself a talking-to so as to allow myself more time for fiction.

Thank you, once again.
Best wishes,
Yours sincerely,
Jack

A couple of weeks went by, then, to my bemusement, I received this following note…

Dear Jack Kelly,

What a MCP to assume that all women are seeking

a liaison. I telephoned you at the office and I was asked could you ring me back?

Don't bother to reply,

Marian Davies

Once again, I replied by return of post (by the way, MCP was the term used at the time by the Women's Lib, meaning male chauvinist pig).

Dear Marian,

Perhaps you can tell me what you wanted to talk to me about. I am sure that we can sort this out. Nobody here mentioned your call to me.

Best wishes as ever,
Yours sincerely,
Jack Kelly

I was shocked and concerned by her remark and I hoped that my prompt reply would reassure her. It seemed that it did. I was really taken aback though. It was as if, during my absence, she had started to change, causing her to act, the trance had clicked in, and then feeling embarrassed and insecure, she had lashed out calling me names. I did see the danger in this, but she quickly felt contrite, so I chose to forget it.

Jack,

Forgive my sudden outburst, but it took a lot of courage to ring your office and when they asked if you could ring me back, I felt so humiliated when you didn't. I feel so close to you because I can relate to the rural settings that you speak of in some of your books. My father comes from the land and as a child he filled my head with wonderful stories of his youth. Please believe that I never tell anyone that I hear from you. I never say, 'Oh, Jack wrote to me today.' My husband wouldn't understand if he knew the way in which I write to you. Forgive me, I have spoilt everything now!

Love,
Marian

PS Please keep writing and I will pretend that it is just for me. Maybe, just maybe, I am being influenced by the crazy woman that we have as Prime Minister. She recently said, 'You turn if you want to; this Lady is not for turning.' All I can say is that even a worm can turn and I feel weird and unlike myself. M

That had happened at the very start of the new season. We had already recorded the first two programmes and I had edited them so as to answer some of her worries through the mouths of other writers. As I have conveyed, I was both thrilled and excited by this newfound way to communicate; with a snip here and merging together there, I was able to be the ventriloquist, making the talking heads on the screen say what I wanted to get across, while at the same time portraying their messages. It was my own creation; I was God in the editing room. The TV was the innocent tool behind which I hid. The sound was my means of pulling the strings to make the words express what I wanted them to say. I was used to writing in code, hiding my meaning in the symbols of the dream world. I had always needed a secret within my creative work so as to stimulate my imagination. That was how my mind worked. Like a naughty child who knew how to appear good in the eyes of his parent, knowing that his real nature had to be kept hidden. The new power that I felt through this medium was omnipotent, which is why I had to keep Marian sweet and my editing had a newfound frisson. It seemed that my musing was paying off because another letter followed soon.

Dear Jack,

I have got to admit to myself that wanting to hear from you has become an obsession and it is making me wretched. I am trying so hard to be sensible. If only you could answer me directly and talk some sense to me, but even that is not possible. I know that your letters must be formal in case anyone sees them. I am much loved and trusted. Being in limbo is driving me crazy, though. I am married to an attractive, successful man who loves me, so why, oh why, can I not rest? Please don't laugh at me; I know that I must sound melodramatic. I need you in my life to fulfil a need that is in my head or my soul.

Love to you,
Marian

PS I ought to be content with my lot and not bother you with my selfish behaviour. I feel very annoyed with my self-pity. M

I decided that it would please her, and that it would cement the hold I had over her, if I were to send a handwritten letter. To leave out my secretary and put my own pen and ink to paper would surely make her mine. I had allowed myself to obsess over her, just as she had with me. My need for her was very real then. However, I knew enough from what Carl Jung said to know that I must tread carefully. I knew that I had to keep her as part of my creative work, not my actual everyday life. It was a difficult balancing act, but one that I had embarked on, so I had no choice but to pursue it. I wanted to pursue it. Marian was completely the right target for my exercise because she was a wife and a mother, who struggled with herself but would not want to stray. She was exactly the female that my imagination needed to dwell upon.

Dear Marian,

Thank you very much for your letters, I really do appreciate them. And I want to reassure you that you are doing nothing wrong at all. And I do know what you are struggling with. And I want to help you to understand that you are not being a bad wife or a bad mother and you are not in any way annoying me. All I can say is that I will keep writing and that the *Show of Shows* starts in a few weeks from now. And I hope that you get through this.

Yours as ever,
Jack Kelly

A few days later, she left a strange message with my secretary.

'Please, tell Mr Kelly that I got through it.'

I was once again bewildered by her message and knowing that the season was aimed at her, I didn't reply. But once more, she was quick to follow through...

Dear Jack,

Oh dear, I really have made a fool of myself this time! I couldn't quite understand why you ended your letter by saying 'I hope you get through it' and not 'over' it. I started to think to get through on the telephone. When your secretary said that you weren't even in London, I realised that I was wrong. However, it has taught me just how stupid I am behaving and I think it may help me. Please do not reply; I mean that in the nicest possible way. If you do and are kind to me, I will only like you more. Please remember that I will always admire you and when I am sane again, I will drop you a line wishing you well, maybe for Christmas. I handle men at arm's length at dinner parties but cannot control this emotion in my head. Thank you once again for being nice.

Love,
Marian.

PS I must stop reading so many books!

It was obvious that she was having a hard time controlling her imagination. If I could get her to listen carefully now, I really did believe that my idea might work. I needed to gain her trust again. Once she could admit to having those strong feelings I could perhaps guide her so as to make use of her imaginative mind. Each day I was expectant when going through my mail, then a few weeks later her note threw me completely.

Dear Jack,

Are you playing Freud with me? Please be honest; just yes or no is all that is needed.

Yours,
Marian

I was leaving the UK the next day on a writer's tour, but I had to know what she was getting at. I asked Hannah, my secretary, to telephone Marian. Listening in on the extension, I heard the following conversation.

'Hello, Marian Davies? This is Jack Kelly's secretary? He is out of town now for a week, but he wants you to know that he got your note. He doesn't know what you mean, what you want from him, can you explain?'

'Oh dear, I don't know if I can. It is difficult to put it into words.'

'Do you want to think about it and ring me back?'

'No, may I think for a minute?'

'Of course.'

There was a pause.

'Well, I might be being too deep psychologically, but he always seems to know what to say to start me thinking. Does that make sense?'

'Yes, I think so. I know it's hard to answer on the spur of the moment. Do you want a reply?'

'Tell him that I hope to sort myself out.'

My secretary was very discreet and made no comment, just, 'All right, good bye.'

But before she could put the phone down, Marian added, in a distressed tone, 'Please explain that I feel as though I have been brainwashed. I mean that in the nicest possible way. When I wrote to him about his book back in the summer, his reply was on different notepaper. The letter heading changed and his direct line was shown. I got to thinking it might be a message – I thought he was asking me to telephone. Then, one thing lead to another and I got in a mess. Please ask him to let me see him in his office, with you present. Just to have to walk in and face him might help to sort me out.'

'I will ask him, but please don't be hurt if he says no. I can assure you that it will be a considered answer. If you ring back about 5 o'clock, I will have spoken to him by then.'

'I will. Good bye.'

Later that afternoon, Marian called back and my secretary gave my answer.

'He would very much like to meet you. Shall I give you his out of town number?'

'Please, if I have the courage to ring him that is!'

The number was given, and then my secretary said, 'Afterwards, if you ring me back in about a week, I am to set up a meeting, okay?'

'Yes, thank you so much.'

'Oh, he said if you ring him, make it early morning or late at night. He will be out all day.'

Marian's reply was simply, 'Okay.'

MARIAN

I must say that I was feeling very concerned about my state of mind. My obsession with Jack had been only in a tiny compartment in my mind until then. It hadn't spilled over into reality, but ringing his office was so against my nature that I could hardly bear it. I felt so angry with myself for daring to step out of line, and then waiting for his call back, which never came, was so humiliating, so out of character. I was confused and I could almost have hated him for having encouraged me in the first place.

I do remember struggling with the idea of never writing to him ever again, determined to break the tie that felt like a knot in the pit of my stomach. But he responded to my outburst so very quickly, by hand and in such a caring way, I felt weak and unwilling to break free. I found myself thinking, thinking, thinking, trying to make sense of the madness and asking myself why, oh why, has he gone along with this communication for so long? I knew nothing about psychology or the mind at all. I knew that Freud had theories about human behaviour, but what those theories were I had no idea. Something compelled me to write down the question, 'Are you playing Freud with me?' and I truly didn't know what I meant. Even now I wonder, was it because I had been like a sponge soaking up all the information from his programmes and his many books? It was just a feeling I had because reading his novel *The Needle* influenced me enormously. The stepping stones of it took me to Jung and Freud and Gide, making me question the workings of Jack's mind and explore the psychological patterns laid out in his novels. I felt that I was on a journey of discovery, a bit like Dorothy on the yellow brick road. It was all so new to me and quite extraordinary. I knew nothing about the mind. Was I awakening from the girl and wanting to learn how to understand and not to just be? I felt baffled and didn't know what I was thinking. I just knew that I had to keep thinking. I felt I was infected or even injected by a force stronger than me.

I hadn't thought about the stepping stones at all until I asked directly if he was playing Freud with me. Slowly, a penny had dropped and I recalled three names that he mentioned in *The Needle*. It was as if they were engraved in my memory and were calling me to follow them. Their call was very powerful; I had to find out who they were and what they were trying to tell to me. I knew that I had to find them in the library. Maybe Jack really had played Freud with me – whatever that meant!

You can imagine my amazement when his secretary rang; it completely took me by surprise. I hadn't expected that and I found it bewildering being asked to explain myself. And then I rang back and she gave me his number so as to call him out of town and he said that he would very much like to meet me. It didn't feel real. It was as if I was sleepwalking and looking at myself as one does in a dream.

It took me a couple of days to pluck up the courage to ring him and I recall planning the operation carefully, so as not to be overheard by my family. Robert was on nights at the hospital. Being a junior doctor and a shiftworker at our local hospital meant that I was alone and often lost myself in my books once the children were in bed. That evening, I placed the radio in the hall and turned the sound on so that my conversation would not be overheard.

I felt calm as I waited for the call to be picked up at the other end, but it rang without any answer. I walked into the kitchen and finished tidying away the dinner things, allowing half an hour to pass before trying the number again. It rang and then a softly spoken man said, 'Hello.'

JACK

I answered the telephone from the tower that I loved. I was writing and needed to be alone. The stimulation of London was great but solitude helped me to focus. I had been filming in Dublin most of the week, glad of the chance to stay in Ireland. Our home there was maintained for us by a delightful couple who lived in the grounds.

Picking up the phone, I felt strangely nervous, even though I was not sure that it would be Marian.

'Hallo,' I answered.

'Hallo, this is Marian Davies.'

She sounded quietly confident.

'Hallo, did you ring just now?' I asked.

'Yes. It rang for a while with no answer. I thought you must be out. Then I tried again.'

'I thought I heard it,' I confessed.

'Sorry to ring so late. When dialling your number, I realised that I was about to speak to a stranger. It's ridiculous, isn't it?'

'It is a bit,' I agreed.

'I just wanted to put things into perspective.'

'Well, you've made a start and that is good.'

'All my life I have tried to be sensible, but this time I thought I was going round the bend.'

Marian sounded sincere as she said this. I felt actual concern for her, so I stressed, 'You mustn't do that. No, you mustn't do that. I think you should tell your husband. What does he do?'

She took a moment to answer. 'He's a doctor.'

'Well then, he must be used to dealing with stranger things than this.'

'No, he's very sensitive, I know he would be hurt. This might help me.'

She sounded like a young sister might do when confiding in an older brother. My heart warmed to her. Suddenly, I wanted to protect her. I asked, 'What do you mean? If we meet?'

'No, talking to you might help.'

'Oh, I hoped that we might meet, just the once, in my office. See how you feel next week. If you fancy it, ring Hannah and see what she can arrange for you to pop in.' I hoped that by saying this, I sounded encouraging.

'All right, thank you. I'm sorry I got into a state.' She sounded apologetic.

'That's alright,' I said fondly. 'It is as if a gear shifts and…'

'Yes, it is,' she agreed.

'It's happened to me once or twice in the past,' I confessed.

'Has it?' she almost whispered.

A silence fell between us. I spoke next. 'It was nice meeting you and it is always very nice reading your letters, but it would be very difficult for us to meet on a regular basis. Your time must be very restricted because of your family and my time is because of my work.'

I paused, and then went on, 'Because of my work, it would be very difficult for us to meet.'

'I know.'

Another long pause, then she quietly added, 'I had better go now.'

I felt the moment as I said, 'It has been nice talking to you.'

She sadly replied, 'Thank you. Goodbye.'

'Goodbye,' I said.

I was surprised at my reaction to her call. I felt an emotion that I hadn't felt for many years. I thought that my life as a successful writer, broadcaster and family man had been going okay. However, this childlike woman had made me realise that I was not satisfied with life as it was and that I had emotional needs as well as creative ones that were not fulfilled. Like her, I too needed to listen to my innermost feelings and recognise what my anima was telling me, in order to grow from my imagination.

I turned to Carl Jung's explanation, for about the hundredth time, that a man must pay attention to the woman within his psyche and a woman to the man within hers. It was even more important than ever that I remembered his teaching. I knew it almost word for word, like a chant; it was the mantra on which I was now basing my working life.

The Jekyll and Hyde in me wanted to help her yet keep her childlike. I wanted her to be there for me, but I knew that I ought to encourage her for her own sake to develop and to grow, as an individual. I would try to teach her and to guide her to a higher degree of intellectual understanding, while at the same time developing even more of my creative side by using the muse that she had become. I was not only Jekyll and Hyde; I was a Mary Shelley, with a kind of female Frankenstein in the making.

Jung says not to allow one's self to be dependent on any one woman; he warns the following…

'The tendencies of the anima can be projected so that they appear to the man to be the qualities of some particular woman. It is the presence of the anima that causes a man to fall suddenly in love when he sees a woman for the first time and knows at once that this is 'she.' In this situation a man feels as if he has known this woman intimately for all time: he falls for her so helplessly that it looks to outsiders like complete madness. Women who are of 'fairy-like' character especially attract such anima projections, because men can attribute almost anything to a creature that is fascinatingly vague, and can thus proceed to weave fantasies around her.'

I had to constantly work hard to remember this advice. I wanted to be a good man but my character was against it. I reaffirmed my decision to use Marian as a muse. I had always found it very easy to fall in love – romantic love was what I was drawn to. To have the devotion of Marian was a gift from heaven. The platonic communication was very real between us, but I knew that I must keep it in my artistic life and not let it intrude into my private world, where my family dwelt.

To meet Marian just once and to take in the details of her face would be very pleasing; it was already fading in my memory.

I was unable to sleep after hearing her voice; it sounded so gentle, so innocent and my memory returned to that moment, when I had opened the door of the viewing booth at the studio, the moment when our eyes first locked into each other and I felt the need in me very strongly. The need to love and to be loved, not as a flesh and blood being, but as a spiritual soul with an unearthly desire that was more than the lust of human experience. It was almost a religious feeling of longing and Marian was like a spirit that I longed to be real. I had enjoyed a bottle of wine before bed but I knew that it was not the alcohol that was making me feel that way. It was an ache beyond human emotion; it was a longing for a love that would save me from myself because myself believed in a higher spiritual love and sacrifice. My heart felt heavy with it that night, as I tossed and turned, calling her name as if part of a prayer.

I returned to the office the following Monday expecting to hear from Marian and to find that she wanted to make a date to meet me again. It was with a sinking feeling that I read the letter waiting for me on top of the pile of correspondence on my desk.

Dear Jack,

Thank you for saying that I may see you, but talking to you made me realise that if I came it wouldn't be to get things into perspective. It would be because I want to see you. I must pull myself out of this state of mind and face the fact that I am only flattering your ego and hurting myself.

Bye,
Marian.

PS How can I just forget when you visit my home on the TV, in newspapers, on the radio and you also sit in my bookcase? How can I forget? M

I was unable to manipulate my interviewees to reply on air to her sad letter because the first few programmes in the series had gone out and I had already edited and recorded the rest.

Dear Marian,

Please don't upset yourself so much. I do suggest that you tell your husband. I'm sure that he would understand and probably laugh you out of it in no time. Meanwhile, please be assured of my best wishes and hopes that you will be fit and well as soon as possible.

On a different subject, I am sure that with your Irish background, like me, you are relieved that Thomas McMahon has been sentenced to life in prison for the assassination of Lord Mountbatten. Justice has been done.

Yours sincerely,
Jack K

The intense nature of our relationship seemed like an electric force through the air, unsaid thoughts being the vital flux between us. Our letters crossed, proving this to be ever so.

Dear Jack,

Please let me write my way out of my self-pity. I have listened to your last two interviews and both the writers were right, I do find myself in your books. It must have made a huge difference reading them one after another over several months. Perhaps I use you the way that women in America use their psychiatrists. I want and I need something that is just for me so as not to be just a life-support machine, much as I love my family. Can it be wrong to cling to you with my mind, if I can cope? Please let me reach out for you from time to time.

Love to you,
Marian (your pen pal)

P.S .You know what they say about women drivers, a gear may slip from time to time!

My reply was immediate.

Dear Marian,

Thanks for your letter. I think 'writing your way out of it' seems a very good idea. Good luck to you.

Yours sincerely,
& best wishes,
Jack

It had been the decent man in me that had suggested that she get help to end her confusion, by reaching out to her husband, but I was very aware that doing so would have had the effect of a power cut. The invisible signal pulsing through the airwaves would have had no receptor to receive it. Thankfully, she gave me what I wanted; I was delighted. However, I admitted to myself, I had hoped for a meeting so as to see her once again. I knew that we would have been reserved, holding back and not saying anything out of place; that was the type of people Marian and I were. Or the type of people that we had been brought up to be, fighting to hold in the passion of the imagination and the struggle of the world within. It would have been painful, most probably, to see each other for an hour or two in a sterile office and only make small talk. I would have adopted the air of the teacher, mentioning only forthcoming programmes, and she would have smiled politely, listening attentively. Or she might have broken down as the repentant schoolgirl when facing the head of year, feeling confused and guilty for letting both herself and her family down (as she would see it) and for wasting my time (as she would see it).

I could only imagine what might have been, but even imagining was pleasing to me and I had her out there, waiting for me to cast yet more spells on her unsuspecting mind. I was in a state of love and I enjoyed it; it made me hurt, as it stroked my pain, and that was what I needed so as to know I was alive. The pain and the sorrow of love meant more to me than the joy, as expressed by the poets. I wanted to feel that I bled from the scar of love; the metaphor of an arrow piercing the heart was so accurate to me. I wanted to bleed and I hoped that Marian did too.

MARIAN

As far as my everyday life was concerned, I was my usual self; it was only when alone and my husband was working evenings or weekends that I went into the Jack Kelly zone. Somehow I was able to departmentalise my two worlds and I did have two very different personas at that time, which I switched on and off according to the circumstances. I must have seemed stable because Robert being a doctor never questioned my state of mind or that I appeared different in any way. He knew that I admired Jack Kelly and that I had a correspondence with him, but he could have had no idea of the conditioning (grooming, as it would now be called) that was going on and that my mind was changing both by myself and by an outside influence.

Of course, I believe in free will and that most people know the difference between right and wrong, so I was not completely innocent, but I was very much the undeveloped mind in the hands of the great intellectual, and although he couldn't force me to hang on his every word, he knew precisely what he was doing and that I was plugged into him. He was the current and he only had to press the right button to switch me on. It puzzled me as to how I had the attention of such a prominent personality, a household name and a celebrity. It puzzled me and, I have to say, it delighted me, especially as I had no idea what was really going on. I admit that it did give me a thrill, switching on the television set whenever his programme was on air. I felt a great connection, and being allowed to correspond with him gave me a sense of freedom. In fact, it was a bondage, which made me far from free.

I didn't feel unfaithful to my husband because I felt as long as I was just a fan writing to her chosen idol, it was okay. The fact that I got carried away in the toing and the froing made me a stupid, lovesick woman and I came to regret that. It never occurred to me that he was getting something out of the relationship until I took it upon myself to explore the shelves in the library and discovered Jung and Freud. Even then, at first, I was only reading them from my own point of view; I had no idea that he was practising what they were preaching. I thought that I was a victim of my own silliness, not a victim of his power.

As you can imagine, I have had time to think long and hard about my part in the dramatic bonding between us and I have wondered whether it might have had something to do with my childhood. When I think back to the days, and they were very happy days, at a convent school where I was taught the passion of Christ and the devotion to the saints, I feel that it embedded a certain yearning in me. I was in a very spiritual world of love and sorrow. I was used to looking up to Our Lord, who I loved and longed for and felt the need to reach out to and to love. Being married was wonderful but the love for my husband was in the real world. I had experienced the sorrow of Jesus who died on the cross and the tender love I felt that he had for me in doing so. I needed that spiritual love – it was very different from the madness of first being 'in love', when the mind is swamped by the heart and the flesh is weak in its longing.

I wonder if the love of Jesus was the love that I was trying to rekindle in reaching out to Jack. I missed the atmosphere of the closeted convent life that was so colourful, so beautiful, so spiritual and so apart from the real world. The story of Jesus with all his pain and his sorrow filled me with a spiritual need, some of which I lost once the Vatican modernised and did away with the Latin and a lot of the mystique of the Catholic service. I had been engulfed by it all and maybe I turned to Jack Kelly and his world of art as a spiritual supplement to my life. I am not meaning to be blasphemous or sacrilegious; my religion remains with me as an important part of my life, but I really do think that I was looking for that wonderful place within, where love of an invisible being is romantic and admiration of something that is higher than one's self is fulfilled.

Writing to Jack was almost like a prayer for me, and his gentle encouragement like the forgiving priest who wants the best for the child. His work was taking me to another level where my intellect could grow and feed. I was weak in my devotion to Jack and I enjoyed the pain of worshipping from afar. If I had remained a follower without questioning,

I would have been like the martyred saints of old, dying for my faith; instead, I spoke up to my leader and offended him. His plan was to cast me aside and move on to the next convert as he left me by the wayside feeling shame and guilt. I challenged him because I could feel myself drowning in the tide of his arrogance. I fought to understand the meaning and I held out against the current of his abusive power.

Also, it was a time in society when I was living the life that I had been conditioned for and one that was changing rapidly for women. I was not involved in the women's movement, being too busy raising a family to pay much attention to it all. However, I was aware of the world around me and I must have been influenced by the fact that the political world and the change to more outspoken popular culture was in conflict. Maybe somewhere in my comfortable bubble I felt that I had the right to speak to the outside world from within the security of my home, as long as I was not actually beyond its confines. I never wanted to burn my bra or to become a man-hater. My experience of men was very limited but very special. Both my father and my husband respected women and were generous with their love.

The fight of the ordinary man and woman in the street, through the power of the limited televised news, was infectious without one even knowing it. My own family life enlightened me with a shock that my children were growing up in a very different world from the one that I was trying to impose upon them and they were being encouraged to question everything and everybody. Even the question of good and evil became unfashionable, and as for hell it was banished from thought. I had been taught that we are made in the image of God and that the Devil is sitting on our shoulder trying hard to tempt us at every possible moment. After my experience with Jack, I started questioning that. I started to believe that most of us are born in the image of the Devil and it is God who has to fight with all of his might to save us from ourselves. I did, I did feel that.

JACK

The season had opened early in November with a talk about writers and in particular North American writers and how they perceived the American dream. The nightmare of failure and the pursuit of success were top of the list, both in the written word and on the screen. I edited the talk to conclude with me asking why some people turned to writers and fiction in their everyday lives and was it a desire to find a solution to life or even to escape from it? I pressed my guests to agree that it was often the case that those who turned to books usually had a problem; they were looking for something or didn't want to hurt somebody. Or it was easier not to change things.

I enjoyed the new game of making voices talk for me on TV. It was dangerous, giving me an adrenaline rush that was like a drug. A godly power that gave me the last laugh on those who had thought me too jumped-up for the plum job in the world of the Arts on television. The following week I talked to a couple of acclaimed writers from the UK and let their words speak for me; they ended by saying that they did not regard themselves as psychiatrists, but that they felt the job of a good novelist was to help the reader to know his/her own nature.

Those two writers had helped to launch the season, and as Marian had already acknowledged that she was on my wavelength, I prodded them in her direction.

She wrote to me:

Dear Jack,

I just want to say 'hallo' and to tell you what a lovely uplift I have obtained – the only book of yours that I hadn't read was *Don't Fence Me In* and I managed to get a copy today. The silly thing is that I will not start it for fear of finishing it! As I read the words, you will be with me. I shall be lost in its spell. There are times when I cannot believe my good fortune, to have found your books, to have met you and to realise that you understand me is quite remarkable. Thank you for not writing me off as a stupid female. Thank you for your support.

Thank you for letting me witter on again.
Bye,
Love from,
Marian

A week later, the programme showed a film explaining the strange platonic affairs between different artists and their muses. She responded: 'Please remember that I am out here and that I follow your career with interest.'

The next week, we featured the music from great classical composers, emphasising the powerful mood of a different type of written word when interpreted by the musicians who read it.

Dear Jack,

I would like you to know that thanks to you and a loving family, I am fit and well. I must tell you though that in the past I used to say, 'Oh, no; not that Jack Kelly!' Your younger image annoyed me – sorry! Please receive the following piece with my love…

'I am always sure that you understand my feelings, always sure that you feel, sure that across the gulf you reach your hand. You are invulnerable; you have no Achilles' heel. You will go on, and when you have prevailed you can say, at this point many a one has failed.

But what have I, but what have I, my friend, to give you, what can you receive from me? Only the friendship and the sympathy. Who has and gives those qualities upon which friendship lives. How much it means that I say this to you without those friendships etc… '

Jack, I have taken these words quite out of context from T. S. *Eliot's Portrait of a Lady*.

Love,
Marian

Dear Marian

Thank you very much for your letter. I am delighted that you enjoyed *Don't Fence Me In*. And I am really thrilled that everything is going so well. The beautiful piece from *Portrait of a Lady* pleased me no end.

I don't at all blame you for not liking my earlier image; I did look a bit of a prat!

I wish you a happy Christmas, somewhat early.
Yours sincerely,
Jack

Then came the terrible news that John Lennon had been shot dead in New York City. I called an emergency meeting with the production team to plan and run a special programme, as a fitting tribute to him, as a musician and songwriter. The BBC gave us a prime-time slot to reach out to the nation. At the same time, thousands of grieving fans held a vigil in Liverpool. The words from his beautiful song 'Imagine' turned the screen into a memorial for the ex-Beatle and tributes came flooding in from the viewers.

For the final programme before Christmas, we looked at the story of Cinderella, stressing how it was every young girl's dream to be found by her Prince Charming. And as it was Christmas, I felt daring; I allowed myself to say, 'Goodbye and a happy Christmas to our viewers, out there.' I looked straight into the camera as I said that with deliberation.

I felt content with this new attraction in my life. I had

been used to living in my mind; now, I had a constant companion living there, one that I could focus on to my heart's delight. I used Marian in whatever I planned for future programmes and I allowed myself to imagine what she would pick up on whenever I was interviewing performers or filming their work. Instead of the wider audience, I zoned in on my devoted fan and allowed my infatuation to grow and to flourish.

Because I wanted to encourage Marian and to show how much my emotions were inflamed by her, I wore a red tie on that Christmas programme, but it was no ordinary tie. It was pillar-box red and it was so long that when sitting it reached my ankles. I know it sounds as though I am exaggerating, but I'm not. It really was as outrageous as that. Looking back, I can see I was in a state of madness. I felt completely confident in my all-powerful BBC television celebrity role. Society had found a new 'royal family' in the world of media personalities. The likes of me were in our prime and our fame and power was at its height. The seventies and the eighties had seen the crowning of what was perceived to be the glory of the face on the box – the public liked to feel that they knew us because we were right in their living room. It felt good to be the gods of the airwaves and the privilege that went with this was huge. It was like an aphrodisiac and we were lording it over everyone, just like the Hollywood stars of the forties and the fifties. As they were losing their status, ours was growing. Of course, the viewing ratings had a huge part to play in our success, but the Arts world was, at last, being seen as important for the sake of the nation.

This meant that we could survive so long as we remained entertaining and not too highbrow. Popularity was the all-important magic ingredient.

My newfound position as a personality in the world of television gave me a freedom as well as power. I was hailed like a prince throughout the London set and treated with kid gloves by all the 'luvvies' as well, because they all wanted a place on my programme. My power grew throughout the industry as I made more and more programmes and promoted more and more of the current culture. I had many admirers, not just because of my work but because of the opportunities I could put their way. I helped to form the thinking of the public as to who was in and who was out of favour in acting, pop music, bands, books, cinema, dance, opera, radio, television – you name it, I talked about it. There was much more to my programme than the hidden message to Marian. She was a trinket that sparkled in the dizzy world I inhabited.

The editing room became my favourite location, where I could mix and play with sound and images, like a child with a kaleidoscope. I put myself out in front of camera whenever I could, too, so as to be seen by her. I became more and more obsessed with getting under her skin in the way that I had allowed her to slip beneath mine. I recall that when I first started on the series I felt ill with nerves and it was normal for me to throw up in the bathroom before each weekly recording, but once I started to concentrate on Marian I grew in courage and, as I have explained, took great delight in pulling the wool over the eyes of the unsuspecting viewers. Nothing has filled me with such excitement since and I know it never will.

My world was very affluent. I was lucky and I knew it. The UK as a whole was in recession for the second time in five years and in August 1980 unemployment reached 2 million. Many MPs from the Conservative Party warned Margaret Thatcher that her economic policies were responsible for the current recession and rising unemployment, but she refused to listen. Even when the ex-Tory Prime Minister Harold Macmillan claimed that she had 'got the wrong answer', she remained unmoved. So, of course, when Union leaders also blamed her and warned that her policies could lead to civil unrest she grew still more determined against what she saw as the bully boys of Britain. She may have been encouraged by the fact that Britain had become self-sufficient in oil at the end of that year and she was maybe waiting and seeing if the economic turnaround might happen.

MARIAN

The past had to illuminate the present in order to bring it alive on the page, just as it had in my head, and Jack did exactly that in his novels. I knew that my father felt the need to leave Ireland, just as Jack had done, but nearly thirty years before. After my grandfather had died, the land went to my Uncle Tom, his eldest son. When Mick, my father, was twenty-one, he said goodbye to his mother and took himself to England to see what it had to offer a young Irish man in prewar Britain. He hadn't liked what the British had done to his country, but he was born British and decided to retain his British passport despite the fact that Ireland had gained its independence. Before he died in the 1990s, he told me that he would never see the day when the country would be reunited, but he prayed that one day it would be. Northern Ireland and the South ought never to have been separated and it was a dreadful British compromise in his eyes.

Jack wrote of his family at such times as if he had

interviewed my very own relatives. Their experiences were so close to my family history that I was unsure where his fiction started and my father's true story began.

Mick had told me that he was grateful for the chance to earn a living as an immigrant in mainland Britain, although he did suffer prejudice at times and saw signs stating: 'No Blacks, no Irish, no dogs!'

However, England needed him and so he accepted the responsibility to fight for the British Army and volunteer when he could have gone back home to a neutral Ireland. By the time he joined up, he was in love with my mother and as he kissed her goodbye at Walham Green railway station, he said to her, 'I am doing this for you. Don't let me down and stay true to me, Flo, my love.'

Three of her brothers had already been called up and were fighting overseas, so he felt honour-bound to join them. He pleaded with Florence to wait for him to return. He was sent to Yeovil in Somerset to be enlisted with the Leicestershire Yeomanry and I know that he and Bob became friends on that very first day. Friends, in fact, until Bob died in the 1980s. Bob was a countryman from Somerset and he was a very brave scout when in action from Normandy to Germany. He would ride ahead on his motorbike looking for the enemy, so as to report sightings of danger. When they were fighting in and around Aachen, towards the end of the War, they made friends with a German family who were near to starvation but nonetheless very welcoming to the two young men, and Bob fell in love with Helena whose husband had been killed. Neither Helena nor Bob could speak each other's language, but they managed to communicate and he promised that when the war was over he would return for her, and so he did. Their story is quite a remarkable one, too.

Jack had written about the First and the Second World War and the consequences on families and the difficulties that soldiers and civilians faced. I had read several of his novels on the subject, so I was glad to find a written account of my father's experience amongst his memorabilia. I wished that he could be with me as I went through it and regretted how little attention I'd paid to his occasional war stories. There was so much that I wanted to know and I realised that when I was a child it seemed to have happened centuries ago. I remembered hearing my parents referring to 'before the war' or 'after the war' and to me it was just a phrase, as if they were saying before bedtime or after lunch. I was only two when the war ended and remember nothing of that terrible time when I lived in London with my mother at my grandma's. My mother guarded me with her life and ensured that I was treasured as any baby from peacetime daily life would be, not one in the middle of the bombing in central London.

My grandma's house had a basement that was used as a bomb shelter by the family and neighbours, because, although it was beneath the three floors above, it had a door that opened on to steps leading up to the back garden. Even if the house had been flattened, it would have been possible to survive down there. They had a sink with running water, a gas cooker, a table and chairs, and a cupboard in which they kept provisions. Each time the air raid siren went off, Grandma feared that I would be killed by my mother falling down the flights of stairs in her haste to keep me safe. A mask was hurriedly placed on my face for fear of being poisoned by gas. What a dreadful time to have to bring a child into the world and take care of her. I felt sad thinking of my mother and how she must have felt.

Everyone on the street wanted to be with Grandma because she made them feel safe. Once she heard the all-clear, she would go out to inspect the neighbourhood and check up on everyone. Our family was lucky and all survived the war, both at home and overseas, but what it must have done to their hearts and their minds I could only imagine. I considered their experience now from afar and realised how ungrateful and spoilt I must have seemed as I was growing up. I had no understanding of the hardship that they all had endured. I had felt to be in a very privileged world of plenty, when in truth my parents must have had to struggle to make a life when peace did at last bring them back together.

I had seen photographs of them on their wedding day; they both looked so young and happy on that Easter Sunday in 1941. They had had a long courtship, when suddenly Mick asked Florence to marry him by special licence, which meant within two weeks. Florence was taken by surprise and she said that everyone would think that she was pregnant, getting married in a hurry after going out with each other for such a long time. He said let them think what they like; he was being sent abroad and he wanted to marry her first. He had told me that my mother had been the sweetest girl in all the world and my mother had told me that she adored the very ground he walked on. Their honeymoon was taken during a forty-eight-hour pass and over the next two years they only saw each other when he could obtain leave. I knew that I had been conceived on his birthday, because my mother had joined him in Northumberland and they stayed the weekend at a pub, just outside the army camp at Otterburn. My mother thought she had eaten some rotten fish a month later when she experienced morning sickness. I was glad to know I had been made before he was exposed to the awful carnage of war. What terrible sights must have been imprinted on his psyche after that?

Reading Jack's books brought so many memories flooding back to me, both of London and Ireland, that it was little wonder that I felt that he had written them just for me. I could relate to his words as if they were my own.

JACK

The new year saw me return to the office around 10th January 1981 but the programme was off the air until a week later. I was pleased to find Marian's letter waiting for me, though.

Dear Jack,

Thank you for your very nice letter just before Christmas; it always gives me such pleasure to hear from you. May I wish you a very happy New Year and also remind you that I first wrote to you in January, a couple of years ago. Never in my wildest dreams did I imagine that from then on I would still be writing to you. How happy it has made me. I heard a repeat of one of your BBC Arts talks this evening – it was very interesting. I always learn from you. As I get older, I am excited by the fact that one goes on learning. I know so little about the things that interest me but I am eager to learn so much. *The Show of Shows* has been away so long, I look forward to its return. I noted before Christmas your reference to the viewers 'out there!'

Love to you as always,
Marian

PS Reading this back to myself, I realise it would be difficult to find anything to reply to. Please remember that I do not presume…
PPS I found the first episode of *The Hitchhiker's Guide to the Galaxy* last night. I'm not sure that it is my sense of humour. M

A week later, we were on the air with two black American novelists. They spoke of life as black Americans and how their novels and plays questioned the complex and psychological pressures on not only being black, but being black and gay. It happened to coincide that very day with the killing by arson of ten young black people in a house in the New Cross area of London; later, a further victim died in hospital. There had been no chance to mention the terrible crime and it would not have been appropriate for us to do so, anyway, but it did underline the problem within society. After the recorded interview, as was usual back then, I signed off by saying who was to be featured in the next week's programme. I remember smiling as I mentioned that Lawrence would be our subject.

Dear Jack,

Welcome back. I enjoyed your interview with the black American writers. They were fascinating. I look forward to next week concerning D. H. Lawrence; I loved *The Rainbow*, best of all his books. It amazes me how both of you write about how a woman thinks and feels with such accurate detail. When I first read *The Golden Chain* by you, I didn't have my own copy so I borrowed a library book. The four-letter word had been inked out, I suppose by a reader; surely the library would not do such a thing? I thought that book very sad and beautiful. Although, *The Needle* really made me cry. Your writing is always very soul searching – that is why I love it. I hope you are fine, as I am.

Love,
Marian

PS I wish the programme was transmitted live!

The next Saturday, I discussed the works of Lawrence and then Hardy with a studio audience. I encouraged them to draw on the theme which shows how love has the effect of killing a man when he must give it up for the sake of his family. Lawrence had enjoyed a brief affair with a married woman and, with her permission, had written about it. It was a beautiful piece of work. My intention was to share this with Marian so that she might understand how I felt.

Dear Jack,

The discussion was beautiful. I found myself saying 'Birth Place, Birth Place!' I could see where your book had sprung from.

Love,
Marian

I knew that by this she referred to my book, *Birth Place* in which I was working out my frustrations with my life. By return of post, I dictated:

Dear Marian,

How nice to hear from you again. I am glad you enjoyed the stimulating programme. Thank you for your complimentary remark about my words. I am amused by the letter prior to the last with the anecdote about *The Golden Chain*.

Yours sincerely,
Jack.

Then, the following Saturday, air space was required for the political event known as the Limehouse Declaration. This was when 4 Labour MP's broke away forming the S.D.P, so that week's scheduled programme was taken off air. She responded quickly by postcard.

Dear Jack,

How unkind of you not to visit me on Saturday. I thought that I was sure to see you at least until Easter.

Bye,
Love,
Marian

The political documentary showed that the Limehouse Declaration came about when four Labour Members of Parliament – Shirley Williams, Roy Jenkins, William Rogers and David Owen – announced their plan to form a separate political party. Calling themselves the Social Democratic Party, they became known as the 'gang of four'. It gave hope to those who wanted a different way from the three mainstream parties and strongly believed in one member, one vote.

Two weeks later, I had more studio guests to talk about the much discussed but little performed dream sequence of Don Juan in Hell, from Shaw's *Man and Superman*. I explained how Don Juan, finding heaven just a little dull, is tempted by the devil to use his imagination. The devil suggests that the imagination is ever powerful and much more rewarding than the flesh. He says, 'You have a mind, don't you?'

Marian's reaction was…

Dear Jack,

Please have a word with Don Juan for me and tell him that I would be condemned as being on the side of the devil for having such a precious secret as you.

Love to you,
Marian

PS I love to see your letter sitting on the mat.

My response was speedy.

Dear Marian,

Your note was appreciated; so nice to hear from you
again. I hope all still goes well with you.

With best wishes,
Jack.

PS Good luck.

I was delighted that she was enjoying her imagination; it was
a treat indeed to enjoy it with her. I instructed my secretary
to change to a plain envelope in future. Not with the tell-tale
BBC that was printed on the official one. I had thought of
myself as playing God when writing or editing, but maybe I
was playing the devil, as I moved characters around to speak
the words I wanted to be heard. The devil was far more likely
to be sitting on my shoulder, encouraging me out to play.
He would find no shame in that.

On Valentine's Day, it amused me to include the prize-
winning painting, 'The Love Letter.'

There had been a national competition and we offered to let ten contenders be seen on the programme. Her letters had come to mean so much to me; I wanted this to be a secret message between us. The painting showed the sender writing to her lover who was far, far away. Her simple reply arrived two days later and it pleased me.

Dear Jack,

I was glad 'The Love Letter' won. It is such a beautiful painting.

Love,
Marian

Then followed my interview of the men and woman who had formed a Faith group for writers. Their aim was to embrace Christian values in their work and when one of them said for a married man to even think of another woman with love in his heart was adultery, I questioned him, 'Do you really think that?'

'Most certainly, I do,' he replied.

We explored how difficult that made the life of a committed Christian and that it was important to recognise that the world was made up of sinners trying to be good, not good people being bad! Various members of the group spoke of multiple relationships that they had had before finding peace within, after meeting their soulmates, and that sex without love was meaningless.

At the end of the programme, I mentioned that another

interesting lady was performing at the Royal Opera House and that we would look into *Lucia di Lammermoor* in May. I wanted Marian to realise that this was quite deliberate. I felt that Donizetti's opera would be a fitting acknowledgement of when we met and that love can drive both men and women mad. Looking back, I wonder whether I was trying to warn Marian, or even myself, that no good could come from the obsession that I was encouraging between us. *The Times* covered the production with enthusiasm under its new owner, Rupert Murdoch, of News International, who had acquired it from The Thomson Corporation. It explained that the tragic story was based on Sir Walter Scott's historical novel, *The Bride of Lammermoor*, and that loyalty to family and marriage to the wrong person could indeed cause insanity. Both the beauty and the tragedy of the words and the music from the opera expressed my inner world at the time. And with the anniversary of our meeting, I wanted Marian to enjoy Lucia and Edgardo's pain.

In the meantime, we continued to play the game of ping-pong, Marian with her letters, me with the programme. Just imagine if we had had Facebook or Twitter to communicate through; we made the best of the medium that we had, though. And maybe our obsession with each other would never have taken off had it been that easy. If there had not been a sense of secrecy and the unobtainability that we enjoyed. I have to be honest and admit that I wouldn't have been attracted in the first instance had I not been able to use my creative work in our communication. I would not have pursued her and maybe I'd never have known such a creative force within. I had believed that God gave Art as a way to express the soul, but once again I acknowledged the devil in me as I took pleasure in deceiving everyone on the production team. I always used what would interest the growing audience, but twisted and turned the end product, before recording to go on air, no matter what the subject.

I felt excited as we filmed the cast at the Royal Opera House and I took delight in the cutting room as I edited the shots, highlighting the parts of the plot that I wanted Marian to grasp. The recording sat on the shelf for several months, just waiting for our, on air, anniversary celebration.

In the meantime, the beginning of March saw a different tone appear in Marian's letters.

Dear Jack,

How brave you are as a writer to be so honest about yourself. Even though you hide behind two or three different characters in each book, pieced together they make you.

My favourite Ibsen play is on TV this week, *Hedda Gabler*, I look forward to that. She is such a strong woman and in total contrast to the real-life fairy tale of our Prince Charles just getting engaged to Lady Diana. Also, I am glad that the film *Tess* is to be shown in this country after all the controversy regarding the director, Roman Polanski; it looks very beautiful. I hope that Diana has a happier life than either of those women, though.

Now that the children have returned to school, I'm going to try to take advantage of the peace and quiet and get down to some serious reading. I have never read anything about the mind, apart from the practice of yoga. I am reading *The Ego and the Id* at the moment – wish me luck. When I want to see you I tell myself how lucky I am and not to be greedy. Please drop me a line when you can.

Love to you,
Marian

PS Have you started your next book?

I replied promptly.

Dear Marian,

Thanks very much for your note. It is so nice of you to keep encouraging me about my writing. Actually I am working hard on a textbook on the history of Ireland, so it might be a while until I can get round to my next novel. I was saddened by the bombing recently of a Liverpool-registered coal ship in Lough Foyle, when the IRA hijacked a pilot boat to carry out the crime, on the border with Northern Ireland. Your father will be concerned, like me, regarding the anti-Irish anger this brings with it. I am trying to explain the reason behind the continued fight and how the partitioning of a country causes such hatred amongst people.

I certainly wish you luck with *The Ego and the Id*!

With best wishes,
Jack

Marian was discovering Freud and it intrigued me to see what she would come up with next. It was but a few days before I found out.

Dear Jack,

What an amazing influence you have had on me; by reading your books and listening very carefully to your programmes, I was led to *The Ego and the Id*. When I found it in the library, I had no idea what it was about. It has helped me to understand that the child IS the father of the man. What a frightening thing this machine inside our head is. I have so much to thank you for.

Talking of machines, I was reading about Sinclair Research pioneering the launch of a home computer, the ZX81. Robert has been used to an office system at the hospital for a long time and is urging me to take an interest, because he says if I do want to get back into the workplace I will need to know how to use one. I checked with the adult education centre, but they say they don't run computer courses for mature students.

Seeing *Virginia* at the Haymarket this week was a memorable experience. Was her mind in a disturbed state or was she just oversensitive because of her art? I would like to see such a play in forty years' time concerning Edna O'Brien who dramatised it. She seemed to understand Virginia well. It's strange to think that I am middle-aged and yet I am only beginning to know myself. Thank you for not deserting me.

Thank you for the anonymous envelope.
Bye,
Love,
Marian

She had noticed that I had instructed my secretary not to use the BBC envelopes any more when replying to her. Looking back I am surprised that I showed myself so openly by wanting to disguise my correspondence. She was starting to want to know herself, as you can tell. Self-awareness would help her, but of course it would take her away from me one day too.

A sad little note arrived a week later.

Dear Jack,

Please let me say hallo, I am feeling sorry for myself today. Sitting here in my lovely home surrounded by love, a horrible sadness makes me reach out to you. Why? This last week I have reread *Anna Karenina* and the beauty of it saddened me so.

Love,
Marian

PS No programme tomorrow – you have let me down again! And Tom Baker leaves *Doctor Who* tonight, after playing the role for seven years. I wonder what Peter Davison will be like – very different types all together? M.

I replied by return of post.

Dear Marian,

Thanks for writing such encouraging comments. It pleases me that you are enlightening yourself by reading so much. I know that it will help you in life. Keep up the good work.

Best wishes,
Yours sincerely,
Jack Kelly

I wanted to encourage her but I must have felt a little uneasy because I signed using my surname, not just Jack. I tried to be good. I did want to think that my work was guiding her to an individuation, despite me wanting to keep her just for myself.

Our letters crossed.

Dear Jack,

At last I think I understand. I could not rest; I had

to read about the mind – I knew that my feeling for you was much more than a silly infatuation. Am I on the right wavelength by reading *Psychoanalysis and the Unconscious*, by D. H. Lawrence? I am not trying to be clever. I am just trying to understand. I could not put his book down. I felt that it had the answer.

Love,
Marian

PS I feel sad reading what Lawrence has to say, in case you think of me as a mere experiment. I know that you would not be so cruel. I do not want to be clinical and probe into why – let me just enjoy this romance in my mind. M

I was truly surprised by her discovery. It was as if she was following a syllabus that I had set for her. I kept quiet and waited.

Within a couple of days arrived...

Dear Jack,

Now that I have had time to digest what I read, I am pleased that the vital flux between us has enabled my mind to grow and develop. No wonder I went searching through the library for the answer. It is sad to be so near and yet so far. I suppose this is the last time that I can reach you this month, as you are not doing the programme over Easter. (What did you say, 'Peace, perfect peace'?)

Bye,
Love,
Marian

So, she had found psychoanalysis. I was surprised. I decided never to reply on this subject, to let my work do that, as indeed it obviously had.

JACK

During March, we featured a variety of artists and their work, from choreography on stage and screen to modern art and even stand-up comics. If the subject matter didn't contain content that applied to Marian, it never really stopped me, because I always ended the individual interviews by editing a few words of hidden meaning to her alone. A whispered message that was said aloud just as the image on the screen vanished. Unnoticed by all except the one person waiting, listening attentively. Always a good protégé, she remembered I had taught her that in her imagination she could hear or see whatever it was that she wanted it to be. She was, at times, like a sleeper waiting to be turned, expectantly watching and listening for the secret intellectual code that bound us.

After the Easter break, I returned to find a letter waiting for me.

Dear Jack,

Just in case you are in residence at the studio, 'Hallo.' I went to see *Chariots of Fire* last night. I loved the scene where they run along the beach with the beautiful music leading the way. I am still enjoying broadening my horizons. I have just read about André Gide in the encyclopaedia, but as yet have not found any of his work. You mentioned him in the *The Golden Chain* and again in *Birth Place*. I remember you said, 'Think on that!' Please believe me when I say that I am not allowing all this reading to harm my life within my family. I would never allow anything to hurt them. It is a shame that I am not completely open about writing to you, but I do mention it from time to time. I do so love writing to you and I keep you a secret in my head. I only want to continue if it's also what you want. I would like to think that in some small way I also make you happy.

Have a pleasant Easter.
Love to you,
Marian

PS It was amusing to see Margaret Thatcher flirting with President Ronald Reagan on her visit to the White House. She is human, after all!

Dear Marian,

How very kind of you to write again. We have many artists coming up on the programme that I hope you will enjoy, particularly the great composers and their lives. I hope you keep reading and find it rewarding.

Keep well and best wishes,
Yours sincerely,
Jack

I wanted her to know that she did make me happy by writing to me and that she ought to keep up the reading. By mentioning forthcoming artists, I wanted to keep her close to the programme. I had to encourage her for fear she may disappear. She was gaining intellectual stimulation and wouldn't always need me. She mentioned Margaret Thatcher's visit to the US and how well she'd got on with the ex-movie actor, the President of the United States of America. However, within a couple of days, Maggie was having to deal with the terrible sad state of the Brixton riots, where the recession had hit the African-Caribbean community the hardest and some 5,000 people clashed with the police. There were nearly 300 injuries to the police and about 65 members of the public. Over 100 vehicles were burned, including 56 police vehicles, and almost 150 buildings were damaged, with 30 of them also burned; 82 arrests were made. Despite all this, my world and that of Marian's remained untouched.

Dear Jack,

Many thanks for your nice letter. I can't help asking why I should be so vain as to think that you should wish to hear from me? Thank you for reassuring me. I really did enjoy the programme about our great composers – what lovely men. I fell in love with some of their beautiful lifestyles – what an inspiration. Have you ever wondered what your work would sound like if, instead of being a word man you wrote music? I can hear it translated as follows. It would start gentle, tender, romantic, becoming sad and lonely, then bold and sensual, but still sad and fatalistic – always sensitive. Please do not stunt its growth and do start the next novel.

Love,
Marian

It flattered me to think that she could hear my music; she was unnervingly close to my unconscious. One interview had been given to a member of the team who flew out to Italy, where a particular composer lived with his devoted Spanish wife. He talked about the early influences on his life and how the death of his first wife had stayed with him. I edited the programme to include a few of his great works before the programme ended. My first wife had been South American and her leaving me had haunted me. Our relationship, too, had been as volatile and painful to us both.

Then…

Dear Jack,

Hallo, I was pleased to have you 'visit' me on Saturday. You were right about the American writer – he did interest me. I agree with his comments regarding ritual and ceremony. The Catholic Church was a very rich atmosphere to grow up in during the fifties, with the beauty of the Latin and the theatre of the service. The English liturgy of today has lost the splendid mystique. Like you, I was intrigued re mankind as 'a programmed virus', but he did not include the rest of nature, so I find that difficult to accept.

Last night, when picking up *A Book of English Poetry*, the page just fell open at, 'An Essay on Man' by Pope. He says a great deal about creation, man, nature and God, ending with, 'And spite of pride, in erring reason's spite. One truth is clear, WHATEVER IS, is right.'

It's wonderful to get lost in books and learn about the Arts. The unrest in this country scares me and the words of Enoch Powell have come back to haunt us with his previous warnings of 'rivers of blood'. The Brixton riots earlier and now more than 100 people arrested and five police officers injured in clashes with the young black groups in Finsbury Park, Forest Hill and Ealing. I always feel so safe in London, but it worries me now for the sake of my children. My sister Melanie says that it's all down to unemployment reaching 2,500,000 for the first time in 50 years. It is worrying.

Bye, hear from you next week.
Take care.
Love,
Marian

I had enjoyed talking about religions of the world; they had always interested me and the idea that man was programmed and was a form of virus was fascinating. I was pleased she had enjoyed it. What more could a broadcaster want than a personal feedback concerning each programme and each subject featured. I felt, in a funny way, that she had become a valuable part of the team. The professional armchair critic listened with only half an ear – to them, it was no more than a job. This correspondent of mine listened in order to learn and to comment on. I loved her for it and she gave my work new meaning. I was thrilled and felt guiltless, conducting this relationship from a distance, through my work, under everyone's gaze. Not even the gossip columnists had a clue what I was up to. They sniffed around trying to label me a celebrity, waiting for me to step out of line, never suspecting that in my editor's room I performed the tricks of the puppeteer. Talking heads, with a cut here, an emphasis there, said what I wanted to convey, as well as having their own meaning. My imagination was having the time of its life, allowing me a freedom that I hadn't known before.

It gave me great pleasure to present a profile, right at the beginning of May, on how, through films and novels, artists have often shown us links with the past and the present. I explored many moving accounts detailing the struggle of poor farm labourers and their families and how wealthy farmers often sacked a man for as little as cutting down one of many trees in order to make a cot for their children. I also showed the plight of a poor widow and how her young son worked the land from morning till night so as to keep his brothers and sisters together. I had written many of my early novels around the very same theme, drawing on my connections with country people and the hard lives they lived on the land.

As I mentioned, I came from Southern Ireland. I was born to a gentleman farmer in 1941, who also owned the village shop, pub and bakery. I had a taste of the good life, but unfortunately our family fell on hard times. I was only twelve years old when the death of my father saw our land and shops reclaimed by the bank because we could no longer repay the loans. As the eldest son of four children, I was immediately kept home from school to work the land. The agreement was that although we no longer owned the land, we did own the house and the bankers, being the brothers of my dead father, allowed us to feed ourselves from whatever we farmed and produced.

The long hard toil couldn't stop me from daydreaming and the sensitive scholarly side of me was deeply encouraged by the surroundings of nature. Tending the sheep and the cows, ploughing and fighting the seasons, cemented my need to express my inner world. I took to reading and writing poetry in the evenings. So, with no formal education beyond the age of twelve, I developed my inner self and by my nineteenth birthday I was very pleased to become a published writer of poetry in Dublin. I moved to England, where I was taken on as an apprentice in the relatively new industry of television and soon showed how earnestly I wanted to learn the craft and become a broadcaster. The rest is history and I consider myself a lucky man.

Receiving Marian's next letter was a joy!

Dear Jack,

Hallo, thank you for the lovely programme about the hardships of country life – how beautiful it was. What a lucky man that you have access to all the artists and their work, who express themselves like you do with regard to the land and its people. The programme reminded me of the traditional folk song, 'To be a Farmer's Boy'.

'The sun had set behind yon hills,
Across yon dreary moor,
When weary and lame, a boy there came
Up to a farmer's door.
Can you tell me if any there be
That will give me employ,
To plough and sow, and reap and mow
And be a farmer's boy?'

Somehow, it also brought back fond memories of my childhood visiting family in Ireland. Back in the fifties, it was another world – one still at the turn of the twentieth century. How I loved it. I suppose because my father comes from Ireland, that is what draws me to you.

Oliver Goldsmith wrote a beautiful poem back in the eighteenth century discussing the move away from the land called, 'The Deserted Village'.

'A time there was ere England's griefs began,
when every rood of ground maintained its man;
for him light labour spread her wholesome store,
just gave what life required, and gave no more;
his best companions innocence and health;
and his best riches, ignorance of wealth.
But times are altered; trade's unfeeling train
usurp the land and dispossess the swain,
along the lawn,
where scattered hamlets rose etc. etc.'

I really thank you for the subjects you cover and for being in my life. My dream lives and grows, thank you. Please remember that it is the month of May. I visited the studio in a bygone May.

Once again, thank you.
Love,
Marian

I received it the very next day and I replied immediately.

Dear Marian,

I hope all still goes well with you. I am so pleased that you follow the programme with such interest and what a surprise that your father is also from Ireland! Another strange thing is that you mentioned Goldsmith, because I have been comparing his work with Hardy's and I am sure that you will agree his work is more telling, although softer, than Thomas Hardy.

Yours sincerely,
Jack

It pleased me to let her know that we thought along the same lines. Obviously we both had a love of the land that went back to our childhoods. By wishing things to go well with her I knew that she would feel my encouragement to keep close to me in her thoughts.

Dear Jack,

Hallo, you are nice to write to me so often. Thank you for your letter. I shall take your advice and read Thomas Hardy's poetry about the countryside. I greatly admire his novels and read *Jude the Obscure* only last week. As I turned each page, I wanted to say, 'No, please don't do that!' It was almost too painful to read. I loved it. What a wonderful gift it is to be a writer. I find it sad to think that so many people prefer TV or the cinema – a book is such a personal thing. I suppose reading is a selfish pastime, though. If I got your birthday right, the day and the month are my father's, but the other way round; I wonder what the stars would read into that! By the way, on another vein, I went to look at Homebase, which has just opened as a DIY superstore. It is quite splendid but Croydon is not exactly nearby, so it was a one-off visit until maybe a branch opens closer to my house. It is a bit like the Canadian Tyre chain that I visited in North America, although on a smaller scale – and, of course, it doesn't sell firearms!

Love to you,
Marian

I continued editing the sound to catch her attention, so, for example, when a novel was discussed that involved a family in which the dad had left home for another woman, I questioned the writer, 'Do you think people should behave like that? I think it's just an excuse when they say it will be better for you if I clear off.'

The programme ended soon after that. By her letter, I gathered she agreed that it was selfish if one partner should walk out on the other. My own marriage was not what it should be but I would never end it. I could tell that Marian's was happy, which made me understand that she had turned to me because I could tell that she was not fulfilled intellectually due to the limited education of her day. The way that she wrote to me meant that she had a lot of growing up to do. It struck me that Marian was the right person for me but that I had met her at the wrong time. Chance had played its hand in our meeting, but I would not have felt so fulfilled creatively if Marian was part of my domestic life. Our relationship was the way that it was meant to be. Jung requested that I recognise her as a very real part of my imagination, though, and to build my fantasies around her; only then would I acquire my quest of individuation.

JACK

Then came my anniversary gift to Marian. I hoped that she would understand that I had chosen Donizetti's *Lucia di Lammermoor* as a special reminder of when we had met, because of its passion, in the hope that it cemented our close correspondence. At the end of May, we explored the fascinating facts about Lucia's last act and what had caused her to go mad. The sound of the glass harmonica was played at the end of the programme as the titles rolled up the screen, casting a haunting sound of longing and anguish for what could not be. Donizetti's music showed the brilliance of the madness of love and how being with the wrong person was the cause of insanity. He was saying that his heart went out to all those who suffered loyalty and responsibility and that to see their true love in eternity was the only hope.

There could be no better tribute to my correspondent than that. I hoped that she would not realise. I was, of course, psychoanalysing myself constantly through my work; it was a many layered, complex operation that I performed for many years.

Dear Jack,

How sad I felt when you left me after Donizetti's 'Lucia'. Thomas Hardy must be right when he says that human emotion is a flaw and a mistake in creation. When writing to you for the first time, I wrote in such innocence – life is very, very strange.

Love to you,
Marian

She had felt my pain, I was glad.

The next week, we previewed The Royal Academy's summer show. That evening, she wrote...

Dear Jack,

I have just enjoyed your programme and, as the house is quiet, I would like to say 'Hallo.' I find it hard to understand modern art. Listening to your interview brought to mind my reaction when reading Freud's lectures on dreams. I was filled with wonder at the symbolism in dreams and wondered how he could know this to be true. Then, he explained the connection with folklore, myths, fairy tales, etc. I accept what Freud says, but have to be convinced on such things regarding cubism etc. I am sorry if I sounded cynical last week by agreeing with Thomas Hardy's view on emotions. Your ending, or should I say your editing of 'Lucia,' was such that I could not but feel sad. The big puzzle to me is trying to understand free will and fate. I already believe in free will and yet fate plays a big part in life. One seems to contradict the other. I wish that we had a secret mailbox so that you could answer all my questions. Do you think a pigeon would be a good idea?

I know that you are still writing about the history of Ireland and that you will have been shocked by the fourth man to die in the Maze prison in Northern Ireland this month. Bobby Sands, I read, is one of four who are trying to achieve prisoner of war status, instead of being named as terrorists. They see themselves as freedom fighters, I suppose.

Love,
Marian

So, she had now found symbolism. Ever since the start of my second marriage, I had written using the dream symbols, so as to hide while yet expressing myself. As she had symbols in mind, I decided to try to get her to ring me by putting a circle before my name in my reply. My secretary typed the letter, then I signed it in ink as usual but with an O, also in ink, before my signature, meaning 'ring Jack.' I would not ring her but if she were to ring me after a message like this, my control over her would be even greater. I dictated the usual formal letter as follows:

Dear Marian,

Your note pleased me. Modern art does take some understanding so I hope that visiting the Royal Academy shone some light on the subject for you. Our programmes for this season are coming to an end soon and not returning until just before Christmas. Reading is a great enlightener; enjoy it.

With best wishes,
Yours sincerely,

Then, I signed in ink:

O, Jack

I was bad to play games but that was how I wanted it!

I didn't respond to her regarding the hunger strikers, as that was too political. It was a very difficult situation regarding Britain and Northern Ireland, best left alone in our correspondence. I was nearing publication of my account of the History of Ireland and had accepted a request to speak about it on Irish television in a couple of months' time. My work would speak for me as usual.

During June, we featured more on the art of painters and their drawings; in particular, the accepted artists from behind the Iron Curtain were mentioned and even one or two non-conformists. Of course, this was in the days before the fall of Communism, so such subjects were quite different then.

It was noticeable that Marian was not responding to my little test, whether deliberately or not. She hadn't rung the office and her next letter made no reference to it.

Dear Jack,

Thank you for the programme on the Art from behind the Iron Curtain. It made me realise just how much we take freedom of the soul for granted in this country. Also, I heard you on the radio and smiled when it came from your hometown in Ireland. I could almost smell the peat fire, hear the evil jukebox and see the gang of tearaways! Did you meet any old flames there? I liked the way you explained that the house where you once went to school is now a nursing home. I have lived in such a cosy little world. I admire the nuns who give up their lives to care for the elderly there. The saddest thing in life is to see the geriatric cases; it seems so cruel that a body that has been strong and dignified, should end up in such a way. Or a mind that has been alert reduced to a vegetable. Life is so short; I am really grateful to you for encouraging me to open up my mind and not to feel guilty about writing to you. The imagination is a wonderful gift and I was afraid of mine until you helped me.

Love to you,
Marian

When she referred to the smell of the peat fire, the jukebox and the gang of tearaways she was remembering my last book. It pleased me that she quoted from my fiction of the days of growing up in the fifties.

As she had still not telephoned me, I thought of another way to test her imagination and to see just how closely she was following my train of thought. I had to know before we went off air for the summer, so at the end of June I used Traditional Jazz as the subject to do this. Three British bands featured and while they made music, I played around with the soundtrack and had a telephone ringing in the background. Then, to close the programme, I had one of them say, 'That brings us full circle to the end.'

I knew that this remark would go unnoticed by the audience, who only listened with half an ear. I also knew, however, that there was a very good chance that Marian would be hanging on to every word, so I left it to chance. And within two days, a postcard arrived.

Dear Jack,

Oh dear, what a sleepless night you gave me!
Bells ringing!
Full circle = O = RING.
What do I do? It may just be my imagination. Gears out of control again!
Help!!!

Love,
Marian

Still, she did not ring. I waited. Then, to my amusement, the following letter reached me about a week later.

Jack

The gears plus the accelerator need a little attention. Due to a slight depression, the matter has been difficult to handle but should be as good as new as things pick up.

Yours sincerely,
M. Davies

I laughed at the fact that she was using her imagination, even though she was afraid to trust it. I had pulled out all the stops to tease her and I wanted to encourage her to pick up the phone, but she was obviously nervous now and questioning her own state of mind. I liked the fact that she was putting the brakes on, even though I wanted her to respond to my signals. I was once asked what I valued most in a secretary and, thinking about it, I answered that I liked to be private and would do anything to avoid a scandal; my office and team had to be unaware of my hidden communication, conducted in a very public way, in front of the eyes and the ears of the viewers. Marian was not the only one to be flying high with her fantasy; I, too, was completely obsessed with her and realised that now she was no more than just a thought away at any time.

Just before we went on air the next week, the news headline was that unemployment had reached 2,680,977.

It was a shocking fact of life at the time. I remember sitting at home, that evening, waiting for the programme to follow, thinking that opera was very much out of the pockets of most working people. We featured a selection of operas, including the meaning of the very human relationship between Nero and Poppea, who adulterously chained themselves together. I edited the recording of "L'Incoronazione di Poppea" so as to send a special message to Marian, confident that she would understand.

The next Tuesday morning, a card arrived and on the front was printed:

'WHAT LIES BEHIND US AND WHAT LIES BEFORE US ARE TINY MATTERS COMPARED TO WHAT LIES WITHIN US.'

Inside, she simply wrote.

Dear Jack,

How beautiful the farewell programme was, thank you.

Love,
Marian

JACK

It took a few more days before my scheming was rewarded, when finally she rang my office and my secretary put her through.

'Hallo,' I answered in a friendly tone.

'Hallo, did I get myself in a twist again?' she asked.

'You did a bit but it doesn't matter,' I commented in a casual fashion.

'I was sorry to let the side down,' she confessed, obviously feeling that she was mistaken to think that I wanted her to phone me!

'That's all right, I don't mind.' I tried to sound as if I forgave her foolishness.

'I desperately wanted to say hallo. I was fine and then suddenly I went haywire about rings and bells and all sorts!'

'It comes and goes like that, doesn't it? You seem to be able to pull yourself out of it very well though,' I encouraged her.

'Yes, I can, with your help,' she replied.

'I do very little, I think,' I said.

'You do a lot,' she assured me.

'I don't always reply, but it doesn't always seem I need to,' I suggested.

'I understand. I understand that. I never want to be a pest,' she stressed.

'I don't think of you as a pest. It is very kind of you to follow the programme so closely. I really appreciate it,' I said, in all honesty.

'That's good,' she all but whispered.

A silence followed and then she said, 'Now that I have got to the phone, I don't know what to say. I feel nervous.' There was a pause. 'What are you up to?' she asked.

'I'm going to a pop concert tonight; we might film Tony Bennett later for the show.' I thought this might impress her.

'That's nice,' was all she said.

'Are you still reading as much?' I asked.

'Yes, I'm really enjoying it.'

'That's good,' I replied. I broke into the pause that followed, 'I'll speak to you again sometime.'

'All right, goodbye,' she agreed.

'Goodbye,' I added.

She replaced the receiver first and I was left with the lonely sound of the line in my ear. I had wanted to say more but couldn't allow myself to. In order to keep my head, I had to keep my distance. To dwell on the thought of her helped my creative ability, any closer and the relationship would have destroyed both my marriage and my individuation. I had to remain the master and she the slave if my plan was to proceed. I knew by saying that I would speak to her again sometime, I would cast the spell that would keep her my captive. I had an idea for a novel and intended to see what I could make of it during the coming break.

Today it is hard to imagine a world without instant communication. Facebook, Twitter, smartphones, iPads etc. have made it possible to conduct a virtual relationship at a simple click. I do wonder whether Marian would have been content with the slow process of letter writing had we struck up a platonic friendship in this electronic age. We were both from a bygone world when the gap between communications made the experience even more intense because the imagination had time and therefore exercised like a muscle. Thoughts were given time to grow and to be nurtured in the space that time demanded. My use of the television was also coloured by the time that I spent editing, alone with my thoughts. It was a very different technology, not at all like the interactive kind today. I wasn't in danger of being defamed by social media in the eighties!

Time passed by in that summer and our family holiday was blighted because my wife developed food poisoning and I had to keep the twins occupied on the beach, away from the holiday hotel, so as to give her the space to recover. I did my bit but the writer in me was more than anxious to get back to my old routine, so as to be alone with my thoughts and my next novel, now that my non-fiction was finished. I needed to let my thoughts move the pen so as to live the life within, which was much more real to me than the everyday business of living.

I realised that perhaps I could never be happy married to any woman; it was the situation, not the woman. The artist's life for me was everything. My wife was very predicable so I suppose I was attracted to Marian's imagination, which matched mine any day. It was like having a playmate, having Marian in my life; someone who would come out to play and join in the pretence. Grown-ups forget that they once enjoyed that part of the mind that so easily conjures up a world different from their own. That is why art is so important to me: the artist can create the world of make believe and move within it to his or her heart's delight.

I had time to read the newspapers thoroughly each day, while keeping an eye on the children. I would sit facing them as they made sandcastles and paddled, but as I read of the horror that was besieging cities up and down the country, it was as if I was reading about a foreign land rather than the UK I inhabited. I'll give you an example of what I read. I am not making this up; I kept a diary note of the shocking daily headlines at the time because I was so stunned by it all.

The Toxteth riots break out in Liverpool and the British police use CS gas for the first time. Riots also break out in cities up and down the country. Forty-three people are charged with theft and violent disorder following a riot in Wood Green, North London. Inner-city rioting continues when a riot in Moss Side, Manchester, sees more than 1,000 people besiege the local police station. Rioting breaks out in Woolwich, London. Further rioting all over Bradford and West Yorkshire. Margaret Thatcher announces that the police may use rubber bullets, water cannons and armoured vehicles against urban rioters. The new Labour Party leader, Michael Foot, lays the blame for the rioting on the Conservative Government's economic policies, which had seen unemployment rise by 70 per cent in the last two years.

All of that had happened within the month of July, in just one month! One bit of good news that I noted was that the BBC had appointed the twenty-nine-year-old Moira Stuart as the first black newsreader. That was a good step forward in my industry.

After the holiday, I called in to the office to go through some correspondence with my secretary concerning the next season's agenda. She had filtered out my personal mail; as I have mentioned, I had quite a lot of fan mail in those days, most of which I answered. I was pleased to see Marian's handwriting amongst them, although I was annoyed by its content.

Dear Jack,

Today I was sitting happily on a south coast beach looking through the newspapers and there was mention of you and a woman they said you like to be seen with. I felt sick, really sick. Please be honest with me if you are having an affair. Please tell me, I could not bear to write to you if you are. If you are, I would need you to pull all the plugs out and leave me to be alone in my self's cell.

Bye,
Marian

Another letter was also waiting, which she had written soon after.

Dear Jack,

I ought to learn a lesson from Gerard Manley Hopkins…

'My own heart let me have more pity on;
Let me live to my sad self hereafter kind, charitable;
Not live this tormented mind with this tormented
mind tormenting yet. Etc. Etc…'

Wordsworth's 'Thoughts too deep for tears…' is also beautiful.

I am enjoying your articles in the *Radio Times*.

Bye once again.
Please think of me.
Marian

I had but a few minutes to dictate a message before dashing to Gatwick, but I felt compelled to answer her.

Dear Marian,

I was passing through the office en route to the airport. I intend working and writing in Ireland and I read your very sad card. There was a bit of silly gossip in the tabloids and, if I were you, I would not give it another thought. I hope that you are in good form and having a happy summer. We will be back on the air in the late autumn and I hope you enjoy the programmes then.

With best wishes,
Yours sincerely,
Jack

I hoped that would put her mind at rest and encourage her. I was angry about the gossip concerning myself and a woman writer. We often worked together, we liked each other that is true, but no more than if she were a male colleague. That sort of publicity really annoyed me.

Then, before August was out, the tenth hunger striker died in the Maze prison; it was the day before I was interviewed about my book *Ireland – A New Nation*. Southern Ireland had a new second television channel, RTE Two, and one of their up-and-coming presenters gave me the chance to put forward my point of view. I mention this here because it has a bearing on Marian's correspondence and I kept a recording of the following…

The interviewer lifted the book and showed it to the viewers, saying to me:

'This is your book *Ireland – A New Nation*, published in the past couple of months. I read it recently and I have to say that I was mesmerised by it and just couldn't put it down. Got through it in about four days, in fact. So, for anyone who has not read it yet, the book deals with Ireland in the twentieth century. There is an amazing account of the Easter Rising in 1916 and the book takes us through the Troubles and eventually into the last few years.'

I gave a half-smile and nodded. The interviewer carried on:

'This is the first book that you have written that deals

with Ireland and the Irish. Anyone who reads this book will probably ask the question: Who is the real Jack Kelly? Is he the darling of London's literati or is the real Jack Kelly a fervent Irish nationalist? Or does Jack Kelly see himself as a citizen of the world? I have the feeling that Jack Kelly is a nationalist, someone who loves Ireland. But, at the same time, there is a sense that he does not have a great deal of time for the modern-day IRA. Would that be right?'

I nodded, smiled and leaned towards him.

'First, let me correct you, I have been writing about the Irish for years in my novels, but this is my first non-fiction account of Ireland and its people. I was calling it *A History of Ireland* until I realised that it is about recent history, hence the title *Ireland – A New Nation*. But yes. You can call me an Irish nationalist if you wish. If I had been a young man in Ireland in 1916, what would I have done? Of course, it's easy for me to say it now, but I am fairly sure that I would have been involved in the fight for Irish independence. It was an armed struggle, a rebellion, and I believe it was justified.

However, the other elephant in the room was, and is, partition – a major mistake in my opinion. The British government's idea to divide Ireland into two countries, a Catholic state and a Protestant state, does not make much sense to me. But I have to say that there is a difference between what happened then and what is going on now. Then, Ireland was a country going through a rebellion. We had 1916 and another seven or eight years of fighting, but those Irish nationalists or republicans – whatever name you want to give them – what they were doing was fighting for an independent Ireland. If we move forward to the present day and the new people, the Provisional IRA, it's quite different now. These people are using bombs to make a point. Bombs! So what do we know about bombs? They kill people. This is using terrorism to make a political point. I don't want to see British soldiers being killed and I don't want to see police officers killed, and I don't want to see anyone else killed or maimed.'

The interviewer cut in: 'So, basically, we are back to the old adage, "One man's terrorist is another man's freedom fighter." Let's face it, a lot of Irish people support them.'

'Of course,' I said. 'But talking to people in Ireland I have the sense that there is not as much support for the IRA as you might think. Most Irish people accept that Northern Ireland exists. It's there and it's an entity. They may refer to it as 'the six counties', but they know it's a bit more than that. They don't necessarily like it. Yes, there is discrimination against nationalists in the North. But the North is there and it's likely to remain part of the UK. Maybe not in the long term, because things change and it might not exist in another hundred years or so. However, it seems that the majority of people in the North see themselves as British rather than Irish. The bottom line is that here in the 1980s the IRA are not going to change opinions by using bombs and bullets. It's not going to happen that way.'

The interview went along those lines and it did help to promote my book. Of course, we had no idea of what was to come and that the Good Friday Peace Agreement would actually happen in 1998. At the time of talking, it had seemed an impossible achievement.

That summer, in the early eighties, turned to autumn

and my family allowed me a fair amount of time to myself and my writing. They could read the signs when I wanted to write and for the best part of a month I got on with it, lost in my world of fiction now that my project on Ireland was launched. Jung's theory certainly worked well during that period. I gave in to my fantasies, allowing myself to dwell on the idea of Marian, and the creative forces within me flowed over onto the page. He instructed never to imagine a fantasy as anything other than real, so with that thought in mind I explored the possibilities of Marian.

At the end of each of these writing purges, I usually felt happy to return to my family, having been allowed time to get close to Marian and happy in the knowledge that I could return to my secret inner world when time allowed. But by September, I was well into the feel of the story and felt reluctant to return to our London home. Life had to go on, the children had to return to school after being at their grandparents with Pauline and I had to get back to recording and editing the programme.

With Marian still in mind, I plotted the theme that should run throughout the season. It was not just my writing that flourished – my work as editor was also helped by thoughts of her. My idea now was to show her how to use her imagination, I had encouraged her to find it, so now I had to get her to use it. Once again, I consulted Jung, who believed that the only way that the masculine side of a woman's mind could be truly developed was for her to forget all about silly thoughts of love; only then could she hear the important message from her animus. He would be her spiritual guide to a creative being. I had to guide her path away from the gentle loving thoughts of me so as to allow her to develop and to experience individuation, too.

Carl Jung's wife, Ema (the German spelling), wrote a very important study on the animus saying:

'What we women have to overcome in our relation to the animus is not pride but lack of self-confidence and the resistance of inertia. For us, it is not as though we had to demean ourselves, but as if we had to lift ourselves.' (From *Animus and Anima*, Spring Publications, Dallas, Texas, 1978.)

And Jung himself wrote:

'Woman is compensated by a masculine element and therefore her unconscious has, so to speak, a masculine imprint. This results in a considerable psychological difference between men and women, and accordingly I have called the projection-making factor in women the animus, which means mind or spirit.'

I was learning how to guide Marian and I found this in 'The Syzygy: Anima and Animus,' Collected Works, 9ii. para.28f.

JACK

As the autumn progressed I became very busy, but I was aware that it had been a while since I'd heard from Marian. I was pleased when I did receive a brief note from her, the remarks in it making reference to a script I had written for a film some years earlier. The BBC showed it one evening.

Dear Jack,

I could feel that you had written the script for *The Beating Heart* and I could hardly wait until the end to see if I was right. How beautiful. Also, I am enjoying *Brideshead Revisited* on the TV. I love the characters and the beautiful setting; I am so glad that it runs until December. Melanie was with me as I watched it and kept talking about the women's peace camp that has been set up at Greenham Common. I know it's all very important, but I just wanted to get lost in the story. I did pay attention though when she said that the hunger strike has been called off after seven years. I thank God about that. Oh and Melanie mentioned the reviews about your non-fiction book *Ireland –A New Nation*. They are very encouraging. I have asked Robert to buy it for me for Christmas.

Love,
Marian

Then, I was pleasantly surprised to receive a postcard on which was the picture of a pile of books being eaten by a worm. I smiled at the sight of this. Enclosed in the envelope was a separate piece of paper with the following Shakespeare's sonnet written in her hand.

'WHY WAS MY VERSE SO BARREN OF NEW PRIDE,

SO FAR FROM VARIATION OR QUICK CHANGE?

WHY WITH THE TIME DO I NOT GLANCE ASIDE

TO NEW FOUND METHODS AND TO COMPOUNDS STRANGE?

WHY WRITE I STILL ALL ONE, EVER THE SAME,

AND KEEP INVENTION IN A NOTED WEED,

THAT EVERY WORD DOTH ALMOST TELL MY NAME,

SHOWING THEIR BIRTH AND WHERE
THEY DID PROCEED

O KNOW, SWEET LOVE, I ALWAYS
WRITE OF YOU,

AND YOU AND LOVE ARE STILL MY
ARGUMENT;

SO ALL MY BEST IS DRESSING OLD
WORDS NEW,

SPENDING AGAIN WHAT IS ALREADY
SPENT;

FOR AS THE SUN IS DAILY NEW AND
OLD,

SO IS MY LOVE STILL TELLING WHAT
IS TOLD?'

As I unfolded the paper, pressed rose petals fell across my desk; this gesture of hers moved me to a strong tender feeling towards her. I had to fight the yearning to respond immediately. Instead, I decided that Jung's principles must be followed and I would think of a way through my work to show my thanks. A few days later, she amazed me, though!

Dear Jack,

I have just read *Man and his Symbols* by Carl Jung!

Love,
Marian.

PS Once again, thank you.

Then, within a day or two, another postcard followed: the picture was of a front door with a rainbow coming through the letterbox. Patrick Hughes, the artist, called it 'Indoor Rainbow'. Marian wrote on the back...

Dear Jack,

Love to animus from anima. I hope this is the right way round!

Love,
Marian.

PS I badly want to hear from you again, when you are next on air. By the way, do you know that the telegram has been done away with as of today, after 139 years of sending messages? They say it's progress! M.

She had got it the wrong way round, but I didn't point it out. I was blown away by the journey that she was on. I felt excited and apprehensive all at the same time. My reply was immediate; I just couldn't help myself!

Dear Marian,

How nice to hear from you again. Thank you very much for the card; it was much appreciated. I hope that you are still keeping well.

With best wishes,
Yours sincerely,
Jack Kelly

It was truly amazing, she was so completely into my psychology and even ahead of what I was planning. It was unnerving to think that I was about to show the anima and the animus in the forthcoming season and there she was pointing it out ahead of me. I went to my cutting room feeling like the bewildered wizard whose spells were so powerful that they worked even before he had a chance to cast them. And who was mesmerising who and how? The vital flux between us seemed to pass thought waves in the air without the assistance of conventional electricity! She had plugged herself into my thought pattern as the perfect apprentice, learning the skills like an electrical engineer of the mind. It excited me and at that moment in time I was tempted to share my secret with other writers to see what they made of it all, but I was too deep within myself to bring it out into the open.

The programmes were already made and I had edited them for the season. It was always a case of presenting the show each week when the allocated time arrived. The team had been busy for months shooting on location or in the studio with me interviewing the subject or speaking over the subject matter. I had the power of the editor to bring the piece alive before the final TV recording of each week's programme. So it was with an omnipotent air of the undercover agent that I sat before the crew, as the camera rolled, bringing my ever-increasing talent before an unsuspecting audience. I was on a high like no drug could possibly match and it was all my own doing. I loved it.

JACK

The season opened with a talk about John Fowles' book *The French Lieutenant's Woman* and its success as a film. One day, while sitting at his desk, he imagined a woman in a black cloak standing on the edge of the Cobb, barely visible in the mist. His home was on a hilltop overlooking the sea at Lyme Regis and the famous timeless scene was written from there.

The story shows how a young woman seeks the help of a stranger to the town. She tells him a lie about her past in order to gain his interest; once he allows himself to love her, she disappears from his life in order to find herself. Many painful years later they meet again, she a successful artist, he a broken man. What the writer's clever story illustrates is Jung's idea of the animus: the woman had to forget all about love in order to develop her animus, so that her creative self might be found. But first she had to know of love. The man, however, suffered because he allowed himself to love a real woman too much. Instead, he should have recognised the woman within himself, his anima. He was already married and a successful man, yet he allowed love to destroy all that. I tried to be subtle when editing the clips of the film, not wanting to expose my intentions to the viewing audience, but wanting Marian to understand where I was coming from. Two days later, her letter arrived.

Dear Jack,

Welcome back. The programme last night was so interesting, because having seen the film and enjoyed it, I now love every minute of the book. There were a couple of points from it that I would have liked you to explore regarding Sarah – an hour is just not long enough! I hope that you are fine. It is strange, but after the programme I had the feeling that you were displeased with me. I felt perplexed.

Love to you,
Marian

A postcard dated the same day as the letter also arrived…

Hallo,

The penny has just fallen! How clever you are.

M.

I quickly dictated my reply.

Dear Marian,

Thank you for your letter. I'm glad you enjoyed the subject. I, too, was a little perplexed at the end of the programme because it was not quite as pertinent as I wanted it to be.

With best wishes,
Yours sincerely,
Jack Kelly

I wanted her to know that I would have liked to have had more detail from the film/book, but that would have been too obvious to the watching world! However, the shock that I had indeed drawn her into my innermost psyche was disturbing; it felt as if the fruits of my scheming would now haunt me, following me like a shadow. She had become my outer ego. I made the conscious decision that by the end of the season I would distance myself, shake off the possible noose from around my neck. I wasn't used to being stalked in the mind and I could smell danger ahead. I had wanted this, but it started to feel claustrophobic because, after all, my freedom was in my creative world and I would have no place to hide if Marian were to decipher my imagination in the way that she so obviously was beginning to. It was one thing to have a devoted follower, a disciple, but not a mind reader who had me under a microscope. I had welcomed her as a muse but I was beginning to feel the need for an iron curtain, once my continued plan came to its conclusion. I couldn't drop the proposed programmes, so I would see them through and guide her along to independence, where she could stand alone intellectually.

I felt emotionally confused as I went about my everyday life; it was easier said than done keeping reality and art separate and to switch off from such a powerful experience. It was all-embracing, a little like an animal gnawing away inside my head, never letting me be. It was troublesome and yet I had to rub it like a sore until it festered. It was a way of knowing that I was alive. So it went on, the bittersweet experiment of the mind, ever powerful, ever threatening, ever testing.

Dear Jack,

Thank you for the Everly Brothers singing of '*All I Have to do is Dream.*' You always know what I need.

Love,
Marian

This referred to my filming of the Everly Brothers and other famous American singers from the sixties. The programme ended with the whole of the song as the titles faded away with the words.

I edited it so as to send a romantic message across the airwaves to Marian. The heady feeling of being in love consumed me, I felt addicted to its power and within its grip. I had, of course, made the filming of that programme some weeks before, thinking that Marian would indeed be flattered by my romantic gesture, but I know that I was becoming more and more uncomfortable about her probing the naked truth behind my unconscious. It had seemed absolutely fine to allow myself to fall in love with the idea of Marian until she became simply a hair's breadth away from my innermost imaginings. Indeed, I started to feel like a hare in the spotlight, blinded by the glare of her enlightenment. I bought Queen's newly released Greatest Hits album that evening and its energy helped me to ponder what I was to do, as it blasted out in the living room after dinner.

MARIAN

I can remember the excitement of what I was discovering about the human mind, and what spurred me on was the thought that I was writing to a writer. I wondered what it meant to have the writer's mind. How was it different from mine, the reader?

I found the notes that my father had kept of his time serving first in England, France, Belgium, Holland and finally in Germany. He had given his diary to me a few years back for the book group I attended to refer to when we were reading a novel about the war. I even turned my hand to writing about his experiences – I thought of it as a test to see if I, too, could write. He had written about his journey through time, waiting for the years to pass for the war to be over. I remembered that he had been sent to enlist with the Leicestershire Yeomanry and his notes explained that several units had joined the Guards Armoured Division in September 1941. He wrote what a raw lot they were because they didn't know each other and they didn't have much equipment or any experience. He mentioned the months of training on the Salisbury Plain and exercises in Norfolk and Yorkshire, where they began to obtain more and more equipment and more and more experience, finishing up with countless manoeuvres on the Wolds and in the south of England. He said that they were trained and more than ready for action for five years, but not tested in battle during the long and ceaseless wait.

As I wrote, I referred to him by name sometimes – Mick. Mick had often made light of being soaked to the skin and the luxury of being able to sleep in a dry ditch when possible, so that his wet clothes could dry on him overnight. He would point this out as we drove on holiday in the fifties, to the West Country, passing through the open, treeless Salisbury Plain. I had thought it just another of his wonderful stories, not understanding the harsh reality and that it was a fairly recent experience to him. No wonder he suffered the pains of arthritis in later life.

The heading on the notebook read '130 Battery, R.A.' and at times I had difficulty in reading his handwriting. He explained that they had waited for five years expecting to see action at any time. All units were on standby waiting, and in 1941 when the Tiger Troop went to defend the Trent from the Humber to Newark against invasion, they wished it had been their outfit that was deployed. That troop was then the only artillery supporting the 22nd Armoured Brigade and under Major Brassey.

The men were getting frustrated year after year when each of the many exercises were said to be their last before combat would commence. Then, in June 1944, it looked as if their moment had come and they were given endless lectures about their journey to France. At last, they came to the first stage, Scarborough, but still they waited. Then down to Eastbourne until D-Day, where they waited for orders to move.

I had been shown the pleasant detached house on the seafront where my father had been billeted. He made light of it, as he showed us it on a day's outing to the seaside. Not mentioning the feeling of anticipation that he must have felt when waiting there. He showed us the nearby Beachy Head, which he pointed out was renowned for suicide cases and I was filled with horror when looking down at the rocks below, but as a child I was unaware whether it had worried him during his time there. In my innocence, I had felt that he had been lucky to be in such a nice seaside town. I didn't comprehend what it had meant to be waiting to go to fight in battle. I had thought it very far removed from my life and time.

When the orders did come, they left at 2 a.m. to be ready at Southampton by 0900 hours and were told that they would only be in the marshalling area for 48 hours. However, their last wait was to be ten days, before commencing by boat to Normandy. They went on route marches to find strawberries by day and visited the town by night. He remembered embarking on the American tank landing ship, known simply as an LST, in the dark on 26 June and that they had a fairly easy voyage, although his notes mentioned that poor old Bill was terribly seasick and that he had even refused to go home on leave the first time it was due, after feeling so wretched. Bill even managed to find the time to bury his false teeth as he landed on the beach, never to wear any again.

The battery's first attempt at going ashore was not successful because they pulled in next to a hole on the beach and it was too deep for them to get off. This meant that they had to put out to sea again and those who were not suffering from seasickness spent the day overeating on American rations. Despite the disappointment of waiting yet again, they enjoyed that luxury after many years of British army rations. As darkness fell, there was a fierce thunderstorm that set alight the barrage balloons and as they disembarked, all the training they had done in waterproofs proved to be of little use, because they finally landed in about a foot of water. During the night, the Battery were split up but they managed to assemble, come daybreak, in some picturesque fields in Saint Martin des Entrees, a little way outside Bayeux. They stayed there until 6 July and he noted that it had been a very pleasant period, despite the terrible reason for being there. At first, the countryside looked very pretty with green grass and orchards and fields with high hedges, but as more and more troops arrived, the land turned to dust, which hung like a cloud over them.

I paused in my writing, aware that my father's voice spoke to me, as I turned his account into words and sentences. It was all very interesting to me, but would it be to Jack when I finally sent him the draft? He would have turned the facts into fiction and created characters to tell the tale, but I wasn't that skilful – I knew that. I could only retell it as it was, no frills.

JACK

I received the following card during the last week in November. It showed a spaceship on a voyage.

Dear Jack,

Hallo, please note this card is meant to complement Neil Armstrong's voyage around the cosmos, but I couldn't find one quite suitable. I thought that the feature you ran on the series was amazing. It was in stark contrast with my sea voyages during the 70s. I visited many exciting places by cruise ships and loved the excitement of setting foot on strange soil, but how I hated being at sea with hundreds of people – being constantly entertained or fed becomes very boring. An ideal way to travel with a young family, though, I must admit. I think the most thrilling sight for me on any voyage, be it land or sea or air, was that viewed from a jumbo jet flying over Greenland.

The beauty of the icebergs is something to behold, isn't it? The journey through the imagination with you beats all other experiences, though. There are times when I think that I must have made it all up and how can it be true? Are you a figment of my imagination? No, no, no, I can reach you!

Love to you,
Marian

Then followed…

Dear Jack,

'ello, 'ello, 'ello, what 'ave we 'ere? It has been brought to my attention that you were seen exchanging information with a secret agent on Hammersmith Bridge. That would explain the picture of the wanted man that now appears in the *Radio Times*! Wanted by whom, I ask myself? Off the record, since learning to read the code, I consider your book *Season's Greetings* to be your very sad self.

Thank you for your surprise the weekend before last – I really did enjoy your interview (anima, animus). Also, I enjoyed the way in which both the spoken and the written word were compared. I loved finding out how writers went about writing who-done-it books, too. I wish that I were able to spy on you when you work. Are you writing? I do hope so.

I am reading my father's notes from the Second

World War. And I have read comments regarding Shakespeare being more important than any man of war, but I can assure you that every man that defended us in that war is even more important to us. If we were all dead, what good would his wonderful and profound words be? I remember Jung saying that the only way to world peace was through individuation; do you think that he meant that each person would refuse to take orders to fight? I like that idea better than Arthur Koestler's in *The Ghost in the Machine*. He says that man must use his mind to control peace – by using drugs in the water system!

As you can tell, I am still exploring the library. You have opened a whole new world to me. Why did no one explain to me that Art held the key to so much? The scientist, Richard Feynman, said on *Horizon* that to understand the world it is necessary to have an understanding of mathematics. If that were true, I would understand nothing, but then again maybe I just didn't have the right teacher.

Last Saturday, I tripped the light fantastic at a dinner dance held at a house that was once the home of Galsworthy. It's a lovely old house and I delighted at the thought of such people as Soames and Irene being brought into being there. Thank you for making me appreciate so many things including poetry. Please enjoy the following sonnet:

'IF THE DULL SUBSTANCE OF MY FLESH WERE THOUGHT,

INJURIOUS DISTANCE SHOULD NOT STOP MY WAY;

FOR THEN, DESPITE OF SPACE, I WOULD BE BROUGHT,

FROM LIMITS FAR REMOTE, WHERE THOU DOES'T STAY.'

Bye, my Self sends love to your Self.
Marian

PS I may not be able to afford to watch your programmes much longer. Imagine, the TV licence has increased from £34 to £46 for colour and from £12 to £15 for black and white! M.

Alarm bells were going off in my head and all of a sudden I felt smothered. Thinking back about how I felt, the writing of Stephen King comes to mind with his book *Misery*. In it, his character, Paul Sheldon, is a novelist who is rescued from a car accident by a fan called Annie Wilkes. She is a former nurse and takes her favourite writer to her remote home to look after him. She becomes irate when she discovers that the author has killed off his heroine, Misery Chastain, in his latest book, so as to move on to a more literary fiction. Annie keeps him imprisoned in order to force his hand and makes him write another book about Misery. As King's story develops into a horror story, Annie declares her undying love for the writer, as she tortures and abuses him. He looks on in terror as she says, 'My God, I love you.' I was beginning to feel that I was a victim of Marian and that her devotion was becoming far too intrusive as still more letters arrived. I knew that I had encouraged her and had drawn her close, but I had not expected her to actually read my mind. Was she my invention or was I hers? Was I still the master or just the slave?

MARIAN

I didn't tell Jack that I was trying to write. I felt that it would sound arrogant to suggest that I could even be thinking of such a thing. So, I just found the time when I could and took comfort in being with my father's notes of what had been a real and terrible world, so soon after the First World War, which had been supposed to end all wars. It pleased me to turn his scribbled memoir into an account of what had happened.

The relentless bombing of Caen by the British and the Americans meant that as Mick and his Battery moved ever further towards the enemy, the Germans retreated quickly from the city. However, the way ahead was made extremely difficult for the allies because of the rubble and carnage caused by the air raids. It wasn't until 3 August 1944 that orders were received by Major Hoare – and it astounded the men. The Regiment was to go forward into country that was known to be still occupied by the enemy. The Major was said to be very angry by this, because at the same time the

Grenadiers started calling for fire in the area where only the day before his men had been shooting and he pointed out that their own guns couldn't pivot round to support them.

Fairly soon, Mick notes, it became clear that the Grenadiers were in difficulty and there were reports of panzer tanks attacking them and large numbers of Infantry. Orders were given to the Major to take an anti-attack role and he and the men were disappointed to withdraw without a single shot being fired, even though it was felt that they could have inflicted great damage on the enemy. Apparently, the Battery withdrew in perfect order even though they were under fire, with a gatepost being blown away by an 88mm shell whilst a vehicle was passing through. And there were tracers whizzing through the trees overhead. Confusion followed because they were not sure where they ought to go and they had to turn into a field in order to turn round. As soon as they were concentrated in this field, they had the 'moaning minnies' come down on top of them, and although they only experienced light casualties, at least four men had to be evacuated. These rockets were not very accurate but made a terrible racket.

The weary Battery had come through very well as they returned to their previous position, just north of Le Tourney. They were very tired but had only lost two vehicles, one being a water cart and the other a carrier. Mick commented that in the midst of it all they were amused to watch as one of their men called Cuckoo got stuck when trying to get into a slit trench that was too narrow for him. As the mortars were falling, a group who were trying to help him made quite an amusing spectacle when they struggled to get him in and themselves on top of him. Even in the thick of it, humour was an important factor in keeping up moral.

On the evening of that day, the 15th Scottish Division put in an attack to clear the area to the left front. They had placed their heavy machine guns in the field next door. Mick mentioned that they had been counter-attacked by infantry and when the heavy machine guns opened up, they all thought that their end had come. Soldiers who were out of their tanks leapt in and the soldiers in their tanks jumped out, and everyone seized his weapon and blasted away in every direction until it was clear what was actually happening. It was a miracle that no damage was done and even that seemed comical after the event – taking the mickey out of one another and making light of things was the only way that they could keep going.

By the next morning, the 15th Scottish Division had cleared the area and everything seemed peaceful after the last two days. In the afternoon, they, the Battery, crossed the river and moved up to St Charles de Percy, where they settled once again in a pleasant green field. Such fields had become like the Dorchester Hotel to them and Mick felt at home in the French countryside, which was not too far removed from rural Ireland. His life between the two, in London, seemed like a lifetime away as he got deeper into Normandy with its green fields and grey stone houses. However, the cold reality of war was quick to show its ugly head again as they soon came upon a large number of dead Germans in the adjoining field. Although it was, of course, kill or be killed, it brought them no pleasure to witness such a scene.

I was filled with sadness as I read his notes, but I didn't

want to tell him that I was trying to make sense of it all as he seldom spoke of the war. I was a spectator glad of his words, explaining little stories from his experience, but it was all matter of fact and I wanted to know his innermost feelings, not just his reporting. It missed out his idiosyncrasy and I wanted his Irish way as he would have explained it to me, but I was too shy to mention my writing even to my family. I felt that only proper artists like Jack could really do such things.

I knew that, when demobbed, he suffered from the most troublesome nightmares, accompanied by unbearable head pains. From then on, his dreams were haunted with him being chased by a man with a gun and the terror exhausted him on waking. It took until the end of the fifties for his blinding headaches to subside and it was clear that he had suffered post-traumatic stress, but treatment was not available at the end of the Second World War for soldiers such as him. There had been no counselling or psychological support to get back into civilian life; soldiers were returned to their families lucky to be alive, and given a new suit of clothes and a hat to equip them to get back to normal life. It must have been a hard adjustment after giving up five years to the British Army and I could only imagine the difficulties that my parents must have had getting to know each other all over again. They must have been two very different people when they started their first home together with me as a two-year-old. They must have felt like strangers.

Many cuttings were carefully saved between cellophane, along with Mick's notes about the war. They were little notes that my mother had sent out during his time with the regiment and she had added a word here or there or underlined a sentence to emphasise her feelings. Unfortunately, they were not dated so I could only guess as to which month they were sent. I knew that he had kept them close to him, in a wallet, along with a tiny felt picture of the sacred heart of Jesus and a crucifix.

A simple note like the following said it all...

Dearest One,

Although we are parted and life seems so frightening, now I know that we will meet again. We had such dreams of a bright future together and we must never forget them. My memories are keeping me company whilst you are away. I pray for the day when we can start our life anew.
I LOVE YOU FOREVER.

Florence.

I was touched reading this I had never seen the brown, aged piece of paper before looking through these notes and I could only imagine what my mother was going through in London then, when she heard that her husband was injured – no matter how slightly. She was working in an ammunition factory at the time, in Hammersmith, and she had spoken of the friendships that she formed there with the other young women who were going through the same difficulties as herself.

Another note that Mick received from his beloved Flo, as he called her, said:

Dear Love,

In these dark days of doubt and fear, the light of
your love guides my way. Like a ship through the fog
sails through the day. Remembering your love for
me illuminates my path and cruel distances is but a
shadow as I fondly hold on to the love you cast.

Plus a picture of a lighthouse standing tall waiting to guide
them home from across the sea, Florence had simply added
'from Florence, xxxxxx.'

My mother, who is such a special woman, must have
been broken-hearted and her mind full of fear for him out
there and for her family, who had faced terrible danger in
London. I was a toddler by then and the future being so
uncertain must have been unbearable.

I found it fascinating putting together my parents'
memories and I felt that I had the perfect life. My family
meant everything to me, and to have Jack as a mentor and to
have the luxury to attempt my own writing was so fulfilling.

JACK

I continued my pursuit of her despite my apprehension and went ahead with the planned schedule. I was captivated by the thought of her. After all this time, I still waited like a schoolboy for her next letter. Although I needed a victim, I could feel that I was as much a victim myself. It was weird, but compelling.

Dear Jack,

Thank you for finding a way, ways of talking to me. I find it hard not to smile sometimes when you get others to speak for you. I should like to read some of Conor Murphy's work – as an Irish catholic, he understands the feel of a religious love.

Thank you once again,
Marian

I had interviewed a lively journalist about Murphy's work and he explained how he went about it. His Irish background played a large part in his stories. I edited remarks very carefully to convey several messages from me to Marian. He explained that Murphy liked playing God by making others talk for him. He stressed how fatal it was to try to bring one's fantasies into reality. 'Is it always fatal?' I asked. 'Oh yes, always,' he replied.

The next week was the final programme before Christmas and I talked about London writers whose work looked back over their childhood in that city and their relationship with their mothers – in particular, male authors. We looked at their reasons for using the city as a stage and their reason for writing books. I edited the show to end with singing from the film *The Entertainer*, to the words, something like, 'You've been a grand audience, really grand. Tell me where you are tomorrow night and I'll see you there!' It seemed a good tease for Marian as it was the end of our season and I had a plan to meet her in the months ahead.

She responded with…

Hallo, Jack, I don't know how to reply?

Love,
Marian

I replied in my usual formal manner through my secretary, just enough to satisfy Marian over the Christmas break.

Dear Marian,

Thanks for your letters. I am glad that the programmes still please you. We return in the New Year. I hope you have a good Christmas.

With best wishes,
Jack

Around that time, it was reported that the first case of Aids was diagnosed in the UK and some of my colleagues were consulted as to the making of a television film to alert the public to the threat of the disease. The Government wanted to make a public health advertisement regarding the terrible danger to mankind. So the year that had seen much rioting and unrest on the streets ended with the black cloud of Aids promising to invade the UK, too. It had been a bad year for the working men and women of the country and now Mother Nature was putting them under pressure, too. It had not been a good year for the human race. The provisional IRA must have delighted in the pit of doom and gloom that the British Government found themselves in.

Over the holiday break, between Christmas and New Year, I racked my brain as to how I might meet Marian without me having to step out of the frame of my work, a way to live out my fantasies while keeping to the rules that Jung laid down. Then, the idea came to me of chairing a programme for the BBC with a live audience; it was a long shot, but I had to presume that Marian would accept the challenge. It was becoming an obsession to see her again. I had teased her into thinking about the idea of me finding her, if she let me know where she might be, but in fact I would be advertising a venue at the start of the coming year, in the hope that she would find me.

My imagination was on fire despite the danger that Marian posed and the fact that I was exposed made me even more reckless; like a scientist working in the lab, my experiment had a life of its own. Its energy overpowered me with a burning consumption that was both exhilarating and exhausting. At that point in time, I was powerless to stop. As the plans got underway for the live programme, I continued to dwell on my thoughts of her and marvelled at how my art had struck an arrow, not only right into the heart of a devotee, but into her very mind, too.

I waited patiently, knowing that the Organisation was taking care of the planning and production of the live event, which would take place in the early spring of the new year. It would take time before we could maybe meet again. The BBC wanted to make a success of this new programme with a live audience, because of the further threat from ITV, who had just launched three regional stations: Central, TV South and TV South West. Back at the end of 1980, the Independent Broadcasting Authority had awarded contracts for commercial broadcasting on more ITV channels.

My diary notes were becoming more political since the summer when I had made notes of the riots. Even in my world of plenty, I was becoming more and more aware of the plight that the country was in. It would have been impossible not to be.

The start of 1982 in Britain continued with more strain

on the Government, and the Welsh Army of Workers claimed the responsibility for a bomb explosion at the Birmingham HQ of Severn Trent Water. It would seem that threats were determined to come from all quarters under the Tory rule. And as if Maggie didn't have enough to worry about, her son, Mark, disappeared during a Paris/Dakar Rally in the Sahara. He was, however, found a few days later, safe and well. Rumour had it that he got lost! My notes for January also show that the miners voted against strike action and accepted the National Coal Board offer of a 9.3 per cent pay rise, but that unemployment was over 3,000,000 for the first time since the 1930s. It was being asked how Maggie managed to sleep at night and I think that gossip had it that she needed no more than five hours a night at the best of times, anyhow.

A fresh year found me in a nervous state of expectation because a note was waiting for me from Marian saying that she would call once we were back from the holidays. Every time that an office telephone rang I thought it was for me and days passed until one afternoon my secretary switched a call through to my extension, informing me who it was. Picking up the phone, I said, 'Hallo, Marian.'

'Hallo,' she replied.

'Happy New Year to you, by the way,' I added.

'Thank you and to you,' she said.

'How do you feel now?' I asked.

'Just nervous. I hate ringing from a phone box. You don't think that I should stop writing to you then?' She sounded so serious.

'If you feel like writing, that is fine,' I encouraged.

'I would hate to become…' a pause, then she added, 'a bore.'

'I don't think of you as a bore at all.' I laughed as I said that.

'I can't help getting into a state sometimes,' she apologised.

'No, it's okay. Anyhow, I hope that I will hear from you again,' I stressed.

'All right, what are you up to?' she questioned.

'I am off to see the D'Oyly Carte Opera Company before they finally cease. They have been in existence, almost continuously, since 1875, singing Gilbert and Sullivan in London all that time.'

'Gosh, I like their little ditties. I'd better go, goodbye.' She sounded so far away now.

'Goodbye, Marian,' I said.

We said so little, once again, and yet it was so much, both of us knowing what went unsaid. She followed our conversation with a little note.

Dear Jack,

I am happy to have spoken to you – what a nice way to start the year. You most probably have a wooden leg and a hairpiece, but I would really miss you now and I am very cross with you for not being on air this coming weekend. Michael Fish, the weatherman, is far more faithful than you. I may have to change my affections! I meant to ask when your next novel is due out. Soon, I hope?

171

Thank you for being nice to me.
Love,
Marian

The new season opened with a visit to Harlem, where Mama Blu Sparks had a dancing school for the young and the old. The music was a lively affair. And the next day, a pretty card arrived of a girl at her first dance. Marian wrote:

Dear Jack,

A poem by W. H Auden

"THE DESIRES OF THE HEART ARE AS CROOKED AS CORKSCREWS."

It likened life to a dance.

M.

Looking back, I am impressed how Marian was quick to find appropriate poems in reply, especially as it was in the days before the internet and Google. She had to know her stuff back then, with no easy search engine to find instant information or a quote.

MARIAN

Dear Jack,

Hallo, please don't think of me as the bad penny turning up yet again! I read your article today – how I wish it were possible for me to write. For a long time, I have thought that you were trying to show me how to set about writing, as far back as *Ordinary People*, it occurred to me. To write is something that I would love to do, but as I cannot even spell, I can't imagine anything more remote. I have started to scribble though, which is most enjoyable. However, I think it a terrible conceit on my part! I do long to achieve some one thing in my own right. Once, I believed that to help my husband, so that he could study and gain success in his job, would fulfil me. He tells me that my success is in the success of my children, but I am selfish enough to want my own success. I have tried to make them happy and independent, but what happens when they no longer need me? They are not going to want Mum to live her life through them.

Bye,
Marian

As if I had no control over my own actions, I found myself telling him that I was indeed trying to write even though I had felt too embarrassed to admit such a thing. I surprised myself by letting him know. I had quickly changed the subject… but I had referred to it.

Dear Jack,

Hallo, I really enjoyed the classical music last night. Shakespeare, once again, says it all.

'BUT MUSIC FOR THE TIME DOTH CHANGE HIS NATURE
THE MAN THAT HATH NO MUSIC IN HIMSELF,
NOR IS NOT MOVED WITH CONCORD OF SWEET SOUNDS,
IS FIT FOR TREASONS, STRATAGEMS AND SPOILS;
THE MOTIONS OF HIS SPIRIT ARE DULL AS NIGHT,
AND HIS AFFECTIONS DARK AS EREBUS
LET NO SUCH MAN BE TRUSTED.
MARK THE MUSIC.'

Love,
Marian.

PS Melanie is worried about the rise of the tabloid press with its huge following. She says *The Sun* now sells more than 4,000,000 copies per day, on a regular basis, mainly due to the introduction of Bingo. Although, she pointed out that it does have a political editor, which seemed to her to be surprising. It reported yesterday that the European Court of Justice rules that schools in Britain can no longer allow corporal punishment against the wishes of parents. She is getting very fired up again because of the SDP-Liberal Alliance and says they are the only hope against the 'evil Tories'. Gosh, look, I am a writer already. All this stuff proves it!

He was quick to reply.

Dear Marian,

Thanks, I am delighted you enjoyed the programme. It can certainly be rewarding to start to write. I am glad for you.

With best wishes,
Yours sincerely,
Jack Kelly

JACK

I knew that she ought not to be tied so much to me; I realised that I would hinder her creative flow. She was expressing a desire to write and Carl Jung would have said that a woman must forget about love in order to reach her fourth and full state of consciousness. I spent a few days thinking this through before sending the following letter.

Dear Marian,

I would hate for you to become dependent on your letters to me and my, alas, occasional replies – maybe you would find it useful to stop writing to me. You might be better off, although I do appreciate your letters.

Best wishes,
Yours sincerely,
Jack Kelly

Her reply was quick.

Dear Jack,

I don't understand. You were happy to encourage me, now you wish to be rid of me, just like that. I really don't understand. I have never let things interfere with my family. It seems so strange of you. Of course, I will do as you ask, but I think that you have been cruel. Why are you afraid for us to continue our friendship?

Bye,
Marian

It was so hard to keep to the rules imposed by Jung and implemented by myself, but if we were to both grow from the relationship I had to keep my distance. I endeavoured to manipulate her through my work so as to allow this brainchild of mine to develop. I seemed cold and calculating but that was not how I felt at all. It was a discipline that I felt had to be adhered to.

Towards the end of February, she sent a heartfelt letter because for the second time the IRA used a unit to hijack a pilot boat, in Lough Foyle. They bombed and sank a Glasgow registered coal ship this time, the *St Bedan*. Her writing was speaking for her already as she told me of what her sister-in-law had informed her about in the following:

Jack,

The likes of me and my family, living here in Britain, are filled with shame. My dad is Irish, as you know, but he fought for the British in Normandy and in Germany. He does not agree with the IRA terrorists even though he doesn't approve of the partitioning of his country, Ireland. Melanie's husband is in the police force in London and he and his men have so much to endure from the unrest on the streets and from the constant threat from the IRA. She says that the Government knew all this would take place and they were shrewd enough to get the police on their side as soon as they reached office in 1979. She says that the Labour Party commissioned Edmund Davies to look into pay and conditions and he recommended a 40 per cent pay increase. Thatcher knew that she was going to cause even more unrest than the Winter of Discontent did for Callaghan, so she built up her police force ready for battle. My brother-in-law is an honourable man and puts his life at risk constantly for the citizens of this country. I feel very strongly that the public ought to be aware of this.

Marian

Of course, I didn't reply to her regarding politics and I kept busy editing the programmes with a careful message each week. I even took delight in making it very obvious what I was up to, by having a woman editor of advertisements explain the art of editing. It gave me pleasure in showing this over the heads of the unsuspecting audience, directly into the home of Marian. I was still the circus manager who wielded the whip when required. The following week, we showed clips from the film *Reds*, paying particular attention to the fact that the heroine pleaded with her lover to leave her alone and shouted at him about how impossible it was to function as a writer with him around. I wanted Marian to understand that she must free herself of me, now that I had shown her the way. She had to express herself in a creative way, not waste her talent by corresponding with me. I wanted her to be intellectually and emotionally strong. I pondered, for a while, on how selfish I had been to encourage her in order to satisfy my own need. The good man in me was, once again challenged!

It was around that time that Mary Whitehouse lost her legal case against the National Theatre concerning alleged obscenity in the play *The Romans in Britain*. I went along to see it with Pauline. It was essential that I made up my own mind on such matters, feeling as I did that work ought to be shown in its original state. Freedom to speak out as an artist, in my view, was an important issue throughout time.

The next week, I featured a pop singer from America, showing in detail how she made use of sound. The telephone combined with, or next to, the television was part of her act and I hoped that Marian might take the hint and ring my office so that I could explain why I wanted her to stop writing, but she didn't ring. I tried again the next week to get Marian to pick up the telephone by playing a song from the soundtrack from *Guys and Dolls*, which was in rehearsal at The National Theatre. The song was called 'If I Were a Bell'. Instead of telephoning she wrote.

Dear Jack,

I wanted to phone you at the office today but I held back, realising that had you wished to speak to me you would have rung me. A man who lives by his imagination would get through if he wished, I told myself. I have survived this last month without depending upon my letters to you! At first, I wanted to write in haste to accuse you of hiding behind symbols, a secretary, a wife etc. I thought of you as a coward, afraid that having encouraged me you would be compromised. I am not quite so spiteful now. I still feel sad to think that you are not prepared to correspond. I delighted in the anticipation of a word from you – it meant so much. The idea that I had about writing was so silly and I have rid myself of such rubbish. I can only write about feelings; I have no story to tell. It has all been said before, so often. I have a successful marriage, a happy family, I work two days a week. I have so much and yet I want so much more. What more is there? Romance? I explained to my eldest son only yesterday that to be 'in love' is an illness that one must recover from.

On a different note, I have just heard the news that an Argentine scrap metal dealer raised the

Argentine flag in South Georgia, near the Falkland Islands, and that the Argentinians have landed today, which could mean war for us. I didn't even know that we owned the islands!

You must be excited about the Barbican as an arts centre. I enjoyed a lunchtime concert there on Wednesday, which was beautiful.

Bye, Marian

PS 'If I were a bell?' I have my imagination under lock and key!!!!!!!!!!!!!

With the letter, she enclosed a cutting from a newspaper. It read:

'BRIGHTON THEATRE ROYAL: 'DEAR LIAR', BY JEROME KILTY. DIRECTED BY FRITH BANBURY, WITH ROBERT HARDY AND SIÂN PHILLIPS. A PLAY BASED ON CORRESPONDENCE BETWEEN GEORGE BERNARD SHAW AND MRS PATRICK CAMPBELL. A WITTY COMMENTARY ON FOUR DECADES OF THEATRICAL LIFE.'

At the bottom, she scribbled… 'It is possible.'

I must just add here that Marian mentioning the Barbican was because it was newly opened at the time, promising an adventure playground for the Arts. How dull and tired it seems now, though.

A couple of days later, a postcard arrived. She wrote on it:

I liked it!!!

This was a comment on a programme in which I talked to a composer about his music. He said how he liked to make himself and his music accessible to his public. After going into some of his compositions in depth, I edited the show to end with him saying, 'People ought to explore their creative life. I am the way in.'

Marian had said that I always knew how to start her thinking, so I hoped that would be the case. I wanted to convey to her that I had encouraged her all that time so that she might expand and develop the masculine side of her mind. I was her way into her creative self. If only she would copy my style, take my books and build her own style around them. She had a gift, if only I could get her to use it.

Around this time, I decided that I needed to rescue my marriage. At least, I needed to put the brakes on before my obsession with Marian ruined everything that I had. My relationship with Marian was just a distraction and Pauline really did love me, even though I didn't deserve it and I treated her like a paid servant. I came and went from her life as I pleased, like a well-behaved lodger. I was financially supportive, I paid the bills, I gave her a good home and I was polite. In return, I expected clean laundry and a good breakfast. I was suddenly aware that I behaved like a free man, a bachelor, and Pauline let me get away with it. She was magnificent in her understanding and tolerance. Maybe that was what I found so irritating and intolerable. I wanted freedom, but I despised it, too. I wanted to roam at will, yet I longed to be needed and held accountable. I was the constant husband who wasn't constantly required to be constant. I had an arrangement with my wife that suited my artist's lifestyle, but I actually dreamt of being accountable to a demanding wife. It was absurd to the extreme, but I felt that if Pauline had been more demanding I would have loved her more and respected her more. The fact that she was so accommodating filled me with contempt and yet I knew that she put up with me in order to please me. I had to admit to myself that I was beyond understanding and I even confused myself. I was a pain and undeserving of love.

Love was what I was yearning for, didn't every artist? 'Love is all you need', sang the Beatles. Love was the be-all and the end-all of what my work was about. I wrote about it, I spoke about it, I dreamt about it. I pursued it, I sought it, I created it and I loathed it. It made me feel alive and dead all at the same time. I felt that to love was to give in to still being a child. I was a child in a very grown man's mind; what good was that? I was as weak as a baby emotionally – that was why I was determined to fight it, for the sake of my manhood. I would be the warrior and slay anyone in my path to whom I felt attached. Not for me, the tenderness of love; that would defeat me. I wanted to be the bull in the china shop, not the lover's fool. I would rid myself of any foolish sentimentality about Marian and concentrate on the domestic state of my marriage. If I could, I really would, I told myself.

I was aware of an overwhelming feeling of anxiety. My

thought patterns started to be very strange and to alarm me. I felt negative thoughts about myself and everyone about me. It became common for me to question my own behaviour and I felt I was two different people. On the one hand, a very able, confident man and on the other a feeble, confused, messed-up individual, approaching midlife and with a crisis. I had heard about the weird happenings to women as they reached their middle years, but I had not expected such swings and roundabouts in me, as a man.

I started to reflect on life and wondered had I had it too easy, too good. When I was a boy in Ireland using my imagined world to write poetry, I was propelled into a certain notoriety at a very young age. Then, arriving in the UK and joining the BBC as an apprentice, once again I was propelled into a good job that got me noticed, and before very long I was a leading light. Within no time I was plucked from the production team and out in front of the camera. My rise to fame had been, in some ways, effortless and I needed to protect myself from a fall. I knew I had talent and I trusted in that, but my reputation was also very important and had to be guarded. I decided to take more care of the company I kept and to try to remember that I had a family, something I so often forgot. I was aware that as a very successful public figure I was under scrutiny as never before, so I would cover my tracks. I remember thinking what a damn nuisance Marian was in snooping about in my work. I was beginning to get the jitters about my own identity and fear that my cover would be blown.

I needed to get under the radar again, but with such a good secret agent as Marian covering me, I was in a dangerous position. Somehow, I needed to score a goal without the back defender marking me. The aim now was to see Marian, one more time, and then knock her off the pitch in a final tackle. I needed to think of a way to break her spirit. I knew that I was mixed up in the head at that point in time and I had to find a way out.

JACK

As often happened because the programmes were pre-recorded, my mood had changed by the time a favourite writer of mine had agreed to be interviewed. He had proven to be an interesting communicator. He described the different subjects and plots that he had written about and I had edited the interview with me giving a summary of his novels, stressing that the author's words should be listened to carefully. His voice was then heard reading a passage from a book. It went something like this...

'As he looked across at her, it was impossible for him to convey his true feelings.'

So ended the programme.

Marian responded by sending a picture postcard. The picture showed a clown holding a large seashell to his ear. She wrote: 'I listened very carefully!'

Once again, I couldn't help myself. I had to reply to her. The clown had a big tear running down his sad, painted face. I was in a state of utter confusion, both intellectually and emotionally. Jung's advice was not easy at all to follow. My resolve was shaky, trying to remember that the creative life and real life had to be kept apart. The imagination had to be separate from reality, yet I had to remember that I had to acknowledge how very real it was, in order to remain true to his teaching and true to myself. Individuation was what I was truly seeking and it was not easy, not at all.

Dear Marian,

Many thanks for your letter. I only stopped writing for your sake. It pleases me so very much to receive your letters, but I am concerned about you. I never meant to hurt your feelings. If it is okay by you, I will only reply now and again. I am truly glad that you are still enjoying the programmes.

Yours sincerely,
Jack Kelly

She responded in a different vein.

Dear Jack,

I have been glued to the news over the past week ever since the Argentinians invaded and the British Falkland Islands' Government surrendered to them. We happened to be in Portsmouth as the Royal Navy Task Force set sail. It was an impressive sight, but it made me glad that my boys are not yet old enough to go. As a Mum, it does seem awful that our sons are being sent to fight for a land so far away. I just had to share this with you.

Marian

We had a number of Russian exiled composers and writers over the next few weeks, presenting both their work and their daily habits living here. Some were small fry, some huge, but all were energetic men; some tyrannical, some affectionate, a few hypochondriacs and all passionately homesick. Many works unleashed the storms of orchestral writing, while some of the writers of the written word conjured up the steely cosmopolitan life of the exile. The common language expressed was of the loneliness of spending life in waiting. I made sure to edit the end of the three programmes with the yearning of that waiting, waiting, waiting.

Marian didn't comment on this at all, but sent a note soon after.

Dear Jack,

The 'Shout All About It' that you are chairing is being broadcast near me in May. I would love to have tickets. I shall be as quiet as a mouse! I am really happy to be writing to you again.

Love,
Marian

So, she had picked up on the idea I had of hosting a live debate with audience participation. I had waited patiently to chair the programme and had deliberately chosen her area and planned it to fall in the month of May, as another mark of the anniversary of when we first met three years ago. As Freud explained, there is no such thing as coincidence! I had very much hoped she would apply for tickets and felt sure that she would speak to me afterwards. I couldn't allow myself to send her the tickets, but I asked my secretary to contact the production team's office and they confirmed that a Mrs Davies had requested two tickets.

I kept very busy, realising that the only way to keep a cool head was to throw myself into my work. For example, I accompanied the crew to Harrogate because the UK was hosting the Eurovision Song Contest. It was very different from the recordings that we usually went to and it was interesting to see how it was covered. Germany won, which meant that they would be the host nation the next year.

Marian wrote, but still she didn't mention whether or not she would be at the live show.

Dear Jack,

Melanie telephoned this evening and sparks were coming down the phone as she exploded with horror at the news that the Conservatives have returned to the top of the opinion poll for the first time since late 1979. Mori shows, she said, that they have 43 per cent of the vote, ahead of the SDP–Liberal Alliance.

She asks, 'Have the public gone mad, just because the Royal Marines recaptured South Georgia the other day? Can't they see that Thatcher only went to war to take their minds off the terrible economic state this country is in?'

She is turning me into an activist, but only in my head!

Marian

I started to obsess, wondering whether she would be accompanied by her husband in May, and I planned to find out where she would be sitting. I wanted to capture her on film; the camera would be turned on the audience, as they put questions to the artists. I had it all planned. I had cast a net and I was within reach of the catch, with a chance to see Marian face-to-face one more time. I felt pleased with myself contemplating this, certain that my scheme would work, and when the evening finally arrived I felt excited. I squeezed my memory, but her face was wiped clean from it.

A girl with a list was positioned by the entrance, ticking off the names of the people as they arrived. Bob, my driver, agreed to stand as though on guard, listening as each guest announced themselves as they were directed into a waiting room. By the time of admittance into the auditorium, Bob was positioned at the back of the stage near the wings. He watched as they seated themselves, then reported back to me as to the whereabouts of Marian. She was with an elderly grey-haired man. To my annoyance, they were sitting at the back of the stalls, so it would be difficult to get a close-up shot. I might have known that she would keep her distance; the seats weren't numbered.

The warm-up went well as I waited to be introduced for what seemed like an eternity, but I relaxed once we were on air. I congratulated myself that I had managed to get Marian out front in a live show. After conducting a correspondence via the television, I now had her sitting out there. I was exhilarated by the thought that soon she would be introducing herself to me. The hour and a half flashed by and I can't even recall hosting it. I do remember closing the recording with happy anticipation, jumping up the minute the camera was off and running to the edge of the stage in my haste to appear accessible.

Many people moved up to shake hands and I engaged in brief conversation for a few minutes. When I looked up, the theatre was all but empty, except for the crew and a commissionaire or two. I remember the feeling of disappointment as my eyes searched the empty rows of seats. She was gone.

A commissionaire walked down the centre aisle and handed an envelope to me. My mouth was dry as I took it. Inside was an A4 white piece of paper and in the very middle, written in her hand, was the word 'HALLO'. I felt deflated; she had cheated me. I had been so confident, so certain that we would meet. I could hardly believe it. I so wanted to see her face so as to hold its memory. I almost did.

I didn't stop to speak to any member of the production team as I jumped from the stage into the stalls. I ran up the centre aisle, out into the foyer and through the front door on to the street. I looked up and down, not knowing which way to dash in my quest to find her, then spotting the multistorey car park I ran like a mad-man, searching every floor in vain. Somehow, I found myself on the platform of the nearby railway station looking intently into each female face as I stumbled along, beside myself with the need to see her.

I realise now that I would not have known her – and what had I intended to say if I had? 'Oh, hi. I just happened to be catching the same train as you. I am Jack by the way, remember me? I am totally out of breath from running after you.'

I was meant to be the intellectual, the man of the world, the man of letters, I would not have wanted Marian to have seen me panting and sweating and behaving like an idiot. She looked to me as her mentor, a cut above the ordinary man. Once the heat of the moment had passed and I was able to think straight again, I was glad not to have caught up with her. My behaviour was further proof that I was, indeed, unstable; I had allowed my obsession to become so out of hand. I felt really ashamed of myself for feeling like a schoolboy – and after all that I had learned from Mr Carl Jung! I had to put it down to my trade as a writer that I was so out of control. That had to be my excuse for allowing my feelings to control my actions. I had to get a grip and to become the master of myself again. I would work on a plan, a strategy to overcome the weak side of my nature. I felt that because I was aware of how ridiculous I had become it would surely help me to rein myself in. I had to remind myself that I was forty-one years old, not fourteen.

A few days later, I heard from her.

Dear Jack,

Hallo, I really enjoyed being at the recording, though I was disappointed that a list of names could have given my presence away. I wanted my note of 'hallo' to surprise you at the end. My dear old Dad joined me; we had a pleasant evening. Have you finished your novel? When will it be published? I am not asking questions so as to press you to reply, please know that. Thank you for your article. I was most flattered to receive it.

Bye,
Love, Marian

She referred to an article that I had written on funding, which I had enclosed in my previous letter. I still couldn't help myself; I had to reply so as to let her know that I had hoped to meet her. This shines a light on the fact that I was not in control, but that she was.

Dear Marian,
I am surprised that you didn't come up and say hallo. It would have been nice to meet your father. I am glad that you are still following the programme, which ends soon, until the autumn. Yes, the first

draft of my next novel is complete and should be published a year from now. I am delighted that the article pleased you.

With kind regards,
Jack Kelly

It was true I would have liked to meet Marian's father because Jung points out that it is the father who influences the woman's animus, the man within.

'It is he who endows his daughter's animus with the unarguable, incontestably true convictions that never include the personal reality of the woman as she actually is.'

Marian must be stopped from developing him too much so as to maintain her softness. I found that women in the media world were losing that side of themselves by moving too much in a masculine environment and being educated above their needs. The essential maternal instincts ought not to be overshadowed in intellectual development, but rather enhanced, in order to keep the woman feminine yet educated.

MARIAN

I invited my father to join me at the theatre because I knew that he enjoyed Jack's novels about Ireland and Robert was busy that evening anyway. We had a nice meal, which my mum cooked before we set off, and I remember being pleased to attend the performance with a feeling of being in control. I was excited to see Jack on the stage but not overwhelmed in any way. Seeing him didn't set my heart a flutter; in fact, it confirmed the feeling that I had had when speaking to him on the telephone – that we were strangers in reality. I had even gone there prepared with an envelope with his name on the front and a folded sheet of paper inside, with just 'hallo' written right in the middle of the page.

I clearly remember feeling glad to have been, but had no regrets that we had not met. It had been my choice not to approach the stage at the end, even though many fans did. I watched them shake his hand as he stretched down to welcome them. His presence was not the same as the man that I corresponded with. The linking of minds was a different world and I was still in the real world, secure in the knowledge that I was being taken home to my family by my father, who I loved so dearly.

When we reached my house, it was good to find my mum babysitting in the cosiness of my home. The fact that I had not thrown myself in front of Jack somehow empowered me. Slowly, I became aware of an awakening and a restless urge, of a sense of purpose that was more grown-up and not only within the hub of the family.

JACK

So all had not gone totally to plan. I had been certain that she would take the chance to meet me, face-to-face. It was to have been the prelude to a very special piece of work that I was gifting to her. My scheming had been very deliberate; my skills so powerful that I had never doubted them. Then that was to have been the end of this platonic, yet captivating relationship. I had been sure that I would have secured her image clearly in my head, before sending her on her merry way. That was not to be.

The end of another season of televised programmes followed quickly and I had commissioned a delightful little film, which was very special. It was planned as a fond farewell and supposed to further mark the third anniversary of when Marian and I first met. The year before, if you recall, I had the opera *Lucia di Lammamoor* as a gift to her, in all its grandeur and theatrical splendour. This time, I was aiming at something a little simpler in order to get my message across and to bring our relationship to a close. The season had been planned with this in mind and, as I have mentioned, much thought went into the programmes long before they went on air each week.

I knew exactly what I was aiming at, even though I had digressed. When I say it was simpler, it was, but hidden within the symbols of the dream world, the garden is where the imagination grows and blossoms. I made use of a film clip from a silent movie with music playing in the background. In a flower-filled garden, a pretty young woman listens to a young man, who asks her if she remembers when they first met. 'Do you remember?' he asks, as she looks shyly away. 'Do you remember?' Still she doesn't reply. The young man implores her to recall how earnestly he needs her and how she had loved him so much, but that he really had to go in order to save them both. I edited the programme with the subtitles written across the screen as he mimed his words with passion.

I felt a little nervous as the pictures and subtitles were broadcast across the air; once again, I had used another artist to speak for me, even though in silence. I hoped Marian would understand that it was from me to her. She would have to think carefully about what was really happening. As the music started, the young woman appeared and sat in the garden, to be later joined by a handsome stranger. Something worried her and what it was would hopefully be revealed. Marian would have to concentrate very hard. It was full of Freud's dream symbols, showing how a woman must listen to her animus so as to find her whole self. At first, she is frightened by what she finds within herself and wants to hide it, but slowly she faces the truth and welcomes what she sees there. Over the last few years, in my work, I had been trying to show Marian how to achieve the insight to develop the animus; the man within. The old 1920s film conveyed this so well without a word being spoken.

I waited anxiously to hear from her and two days later a large card arrived. The picture was of a young woman surrounded by beautiful flowers in her garden. Inside, she wrote:

Dear Jack,

May I really believe that Saturday's programme was contrived on my behalf? Dare I be so conceited? I enjoyed every minute of it, but is it not too presumptuous to even say thank you? How clever you are! How wicked! How naughty! How nice! I had to work hard on analysing the programme to work out what the symbolism was all about. Thank you for helping me to cultivate my own garden.

Love to you,
Marian.

PS 'There was a little girl who had a little curl right in the middle of her forehead; when she was good, she was very, very good, but when she was bad, she was horrid.' My dad used to recite that to me… Bye,
M

In my work as a writer and editor, I constantly looked at the dictionary of dreams which quoted the following: GARDEN: 'The inner life of the individual with its flowers and fruits. Aspects of his/her personality that he/she is cultivating. The various qualities of the dreamer's mind may be represented and the dream may indicate what is being neglected. The colours of the flowers, for example, could indicate the senses, the feelings, the intellect or the intuitions. The garden may be orderly or disorderly; and so may the mind. If it is arranged in regular patterns, squares or circles. If it is overgrown with brambles or choked with weeds; certain features of the character are not likely to thrive in such circumstances. If the garden is unkempt, this may reflect the dreamer's former disappointments and fear of disappointment.'

Marian had understood. I felt pleased and at the same time guilty because I had calculated everything, using her to add meaning to my work. I'd had a great time at her expense, which was why I had tried to distance myself by suggesting that she stop writing to me. As I explained, she was good for my creative career; I could only be good for her if she could rid herself of any romantic idea that she might have about me. My intended plan was for her to realise that she was to stand alone after that little silent movie was shown. I hadn't thought long term or that she might have a problem shaking herself free of me, or that I too would have become so involved.

The season ended with a fittingly gloomy reflection to my mood, as poetry of the darker side of the human condition was read. My beautiful experiment had a flaw, just like reality, and I had to admit that playing with another person's life had been a selfish indulgence, but in many ways I was not responsible for her magnetic mind. How could I have known from the start how successful my experiment would be?

MARIAN

Early in June, I found myself sitting in the garden with pen and paper. To my own surprise, I found some words to string together. I remember that it was a beautiful summer's day and I had felt inspired by an energy in its brightness...

'Sitting under the willow tree thinking about my life;

What it is to be somebody's Mother, somebody's wife.

It is fine to have brought forth children to cherish and to care;

But at times it is so demanding I ask 'what am I doing there?'

The 'I' that is me is often very much aware of the Self that must remain hidden.

Please let me realise my freedom through my soul and through my brain,

The body must be a prisoner but the mind
needs no ball, no chain.

The wife faithful and domestic, the Mother
kind though an autocrat;

The Self lives in the imagination – nobody
owns that.

In my imagination I tackle amazing feats, my
pursuit of excellence unending

as I discover the man in my streets.'

For some reason, I sent it off to Jack, like a child proud of
her homework, adding, 'Please excuse my indulgent little
ditty; the beauty of this day must have gone to my head. M'

JACK

It was bittersweet to see her developing her verse; my brainchild was growing under my guidance. Her verse, though far from good, was not bad at all. I had groomed her, not knowing that the internet would one day be available to many to do far worse things than me. It was a bonus for all the solitary hours I had spent creating an artist out of my own Art.

Although off the air for the summer, I had plenty to do in preparation for the next season, but the peculiar relationship between Marian and I was far more compelling, as I've said, than any normal affair. I had always valued the life within my head far more than reality. I played the role expected of me, chance had seen to that, but at the same time I hugged my fantasy to me. I dwelt on it; she was no more than a thought away; her letters keeping me going, as a draught to a flame. The end had not taken place, as I had assumed it would. I had expected the final curtain and to bow out with the close of the silent movie. That it would be done and dusted, but we were both in too deep for that. I was in the lucky position of being able to sneak off to write whenever the urge came over me. Never before had words flowed so easily from my pen. Every so often I read and reread the wave of letters that had flooded in from Marian over the years. As I wrote, it was her voice that whispered in my ear and I had already decided on the next title, so as to please her.

I received a couple of letters from her referring only to the fact that the Falklands War had ended and how terrible it was that so many lives had been lost and how the Government was benefiting from the victory because the public was, in the main, behind them. A Mori poll showed that 51 per cent approved of the war and that the Conservatives were most likely to win in the general election the next summer. Also, she mentioned the Provisional IRA killing eight soldiers and wounding forty-seven people and their causing the death of seven horses by planting two bombs in central London.

She did also write a friendly letter regarding Pope John Paul II's visit to London, which made him the first reigning pontiff to ever do so. His historic meeting with the Queen, as the head of the Church of England, and then his visit to Canterbury pleased her, too. She suggested that it was a pity that the Roman Catholic Church had lost all its beautiful buildings since the time of Henry VIII and his break with Rome. She pointed out that his case for divorcing his first wife because she couldn't produce a male heir was rather a pathetic excuse and that we now know that it is the male sperm that determines the sex of the unborn baby anyway. She said that she was proud to take her four children to welcome the Pope, amongst the crowds who waved him on.

Then, towards the end of June, a change in Marian took me by surprise once more.

Dear Jack,

I feel that I have been used. What right do writers or broadcasters have to influence people's minds? Who are they except people who put themselves in the right place at the right time? No more, no less. I was so simple-minded that I played right into your hands. How stupid I have been. A famous man like you must have many silly women writing to him.

Marian

I took some comfort from this outburst because it helped my weak resolve to end our relationship. It had more than run its course and had been an experience that neither of us would ever forget. However, to my dismay, she quickly followed with a tender letter in a couple of days. She was obviously confused and maybe frightened by her own feelings. The battle she fought still played ping-pong after all those years.

Dear Jack,

Please forgive my letter of two days ago. Most days I can play the game and it is fun!

Forgive me.

Marian

I was glad to get away on holiday with my family, out of her reach. I even began to feel hostile towards her, a trifle bored. My mood changed and, with it, the feeling of infatuation turned to dislike, I determined to rid my life of her. Jung warns man 'not to be taken in by an unreal dream of love, happiness and maternal warmth; a dream that takes him away from reality.' Once again, I acknowledged the fact that I had projected my romantic fantasies on to Marian who, although very real, could never be in my reality. Just in time, I was able to switch to the inner voice of reason and I listened to the guide within my unconscious, in time to save myself from her clinging demands.

Thus, I started back at the office with a new determination. I would no longer play an intellectual game, even for the sake of my art. Marian really would have to find her own way forward without me.

More verses that she had mused over awaited me on my return in September and I disliked them intensely, the sight of her handwriting now brought up an anger in me that was close to hatred. This thing that I had encouraged vexed me now beyond compare and I felt stifled by the very look of her name. I remember loosening my tie as if to breathe more freely as I sat down to read what was before me.

1. How lustily I allowed you to penetrate my brain
as though you were my lover and I enjoyed the pain.

Deeper and deeper we both explored until the unconscious could not be ignored.

How frightened I was at the start but you understood that it was in my head not even my heart.

Stand back from your childhood and look from afar, you must go back to see who you are.

I now see me and I understand, thank you for guiding my hand.

The me I see is not all nice but less superficial without that sugar and spice.

If I listen to the prompting from my mind, perhaps I can do something before it's too late, to guide my destiny and shape my own fate.

To go through life in a blind man's bluff is oh so cosy but it's not enough.

I will try very hard to do as you bid, so as not to waste the hard work we both did.

2. Your child was conceived with the seed from your sperm,

at the same moment in time you gave birth to your book,

the words that were germinated from our first look

It was only your body that gave her your son,

I consider the art and the act to be as one.

3. As individuals we stand alone despite family and home.

The island that we inhabit deserted even though we learn the social habits,

to please, to care and even to love.
But who really knows what goes on within,
the face shows the world only a mask
to get through life is a very hard task?

4. My letter of yesterday was not very nice
I wanted to hurt you and to be unkind.
The mood that was in me was like a terrible rage,
the characters moving in my head as though on a
stage.
The demon within got the better of me, turning the
woman who is gentle and kind into a he!

5. When I was a child I was taught to be nice,
to be seen and not to be heard;
I listened respectfully and took advice.
As I grew up, I tried hard to serve and to do as I
was bid
To do and to say only what others would wish.
How unkind it was to programme me so
Not to allow my own feelings to show.
Too late I have realised that I too have a mind,
Too late to make use of it, I should have stayed
blind.
My family are used to me always there,
How can I make a career without letting them
down?
I so badly need to fulfil the desire to explore the
world beyond the house,
I have more to offer than to be a dormouse.

6. Sadness is a very beautiful and selfish emotion
the pain like a vitamin feeds the soul.
Most people experience sorrow, boredom, regret
and remorse,
These are quite different from sadness, I know.
To be sad is to be isolated within your own head,
feeling the hurt and almost wishing to be dead.
But to be dead would only ease the pain
and you want to experience it again and again.
That terrible feeling that is hard to swallow,
deeper and deeper you want to wallow;
self-pity engulfing you, there can be no tomorrow.
To be happy is a fleeting thing, but to be sad is
endless if you play the game right.
It can be your very own secret, no one need know.
The mask of everyday living fits very tight.

7. I want to see you and to talk to you
but the rules of society do not allow.
Why should it be wrong or sordid to meet a kind
friend?
Does difference of sex immediately forbid any
friendship just because of what
Adam and Eve once did?

8. Your head is full of such interesting things,
about life and people and this and that.
Please help me to understand how to use my words
as wings.

9. Fear of the unknown made it a difficult birth,
Holding back she fought against nature for all she
was worth.
Many long days hard labour and then a tender
emotion
between Mother and Child, but guilt set in the very
next day,
once again Mother Nature wanted things her own
way.
Her breasts leaking with the liquid of life she felt
like an animal instead of a wife.
On weaning her child she experienced the need to
be free;
Yoga helped to stimulate and relax her, enabled her
to find her identity.
The experience awakened within her an unending
need, fulfilment
Through knowledge and the pursuit of excellence
behind her every deed.
Union of mind and body had to be weaved if action
and initiative were ever to be achieved.
The world of books became her escape, broadening
her horizons within her landscape.
'Return to your childhood and look from afar, you
must go back to see who you are.'
The words of Jung and Freud filled her head,
they helped her how to live, even though they
themselves were dead.

10. How strange that we ordinary people look to the

world of fiction for our escape,
while the man of letters looks to us for inspiration to colour his landscape.
We who are busy living life cannot see the drama.
It takes a vain and conceited mind to exploit the ordinary by making them blind.
He takes their imagination within his hand and shows them glimpses of the Promised Land.
'How clever he is!' we all exclaim
Quite forgetting that he has taken advantage while making his name
as he writes his words seeking his fame, who is he after all?
A man with a plan to shape his own fate, not caring to explain that we the ordinary, we the plain, dwell within his domain.

11. If I could I would not be good,
I would run amok like a local hood.
Where does it get you the noble life,
you still end up dead when the blood leaves the head?
It is in the head the need for right or wrong
and how you are judged when you are gone.
We are conditioned long before birth
so what hope is there for the Universe?
Try as we may for original thought
The pre-historic ancestor still has his way
and returns in the unconscious day after day.

With these verses, Marian enclosed a note saying:

Dear Jack,

Although my verse is not very good, I will try to improve it to show that something has come out of my admiration for your work. By the way, Proust is helping me to understand still more!

Marian

I read through Marian's verse and I didn't like the direction that her mind was going in. It was one thing to have a devoted fan, but I hadn't reckoned on the power of individuation and how my work could influence her thought patterns in such a way. She was becoming a victim of my success, all be it a willing one, and she was in danger of growing too big for the small world that she inhabited. Seeing her handwriting did unnerve me, because I could see that I had been a fool to think that I could fulfil myself while at the same time encourage a married woman to develop herself, regardless of what it might do to her mind and, in turn, her life. I felt contrite. I could have replied offering advice to her, but I had gone too far in bringing her out of her comfort zone. I had to let her go, make her go. The fact that she mentioned Marcel Proust disturbed me, too. It was yet another piece of the jigsaw of my mind that she had pieced together. She had read all the signs that I had posted within my books, finding her way to the core of my intellect. She had unravelled yet another writer who had inspired my work. Jung, Freud, Gide, Lawrence and now Proust. I didn't like her seeing into my very soul. Nobody had ever paid me so much attention before – I had hidden in my secret world – and yet this complete stranger had pieced together the very core of my being and I was naked.

I didn't reply to any of this, believing that time would reveal to me the best course of action. I was witnessing the coming to life of my new creation and it perplexed me because she was in danger of not following my instructions and would then be a loose cannon that would endanger both her own family life and mine, and more importantly my career! I felt threatened again, so I didn't even acknowledge that I had received her verse. I was aware that I was being cruel and it was deliberate.

Then, she laid it on even thicker in her next note.

Dear Jack,

Proust is helping me to understand more and more!

Love, Marian

PS 'GRIN ASLEEP!'

Marcel Proust had taught me to use my memory and to look to the inner world for my imaginings. He said to express the unconscious world would interest someone, somewhere. He also believed that if, as a reader you enjoyed and admired a particular writer, the next thing was to feel that you could do as well or even better yourself. Marian was doing just that; she was trying to be productive. However, by telling me that she had found Proust was like saying to me she had sliced open my mind and could see the mechanisms ticking away. I was truly fearful, when I ought to have been flattered. There was no cause to celebrate that my experiment was succeeding beyond my wildest hopes and expectations. I started to feel like a condemned man!

It didn't take a brain surgeon to rearrange the letters from GRIN ASLEEP to PLEASE RING. She was getting her own back for my teasing her with bells ringing etc. I can honestly say that I would gladly have rung her – but not her phone, her neck! My mind worked overtime thinking how I could get rid of her. I couldn't write her a rude letter – I had to think of a subtle way. I decided that the best course of action would be no action. Surely she would give up writing to me if I blanked her.

However, a postcard soon arrived from her, full of sarcasm.

Jack,

How very kind of you to spare two minutes of your time – it would have meant so much!

Marian

If I had thought to silence her, I was mistaken, as inevitably another letter quickly followed.

Dear Jack,

I am really hurt with the way in which you have handled the situation. I know that you are living out your fantasies in a creative way, so as to reach your full potential, which is fine. But please don't tell me that you stopped writing for my sake. If only you were prepared to give just a little bit more. Why should you, though? You have everything going for you. Given the right encouragement, I might have reached my potential. I will always need more than my family in my life, but they are in my life. I must protect my marriage.

Help me,

Marian

PS Please grant me an interview in your office for a chat face-to-face and with a bit of luck we won't even like each other. You have plenty of heavies in your employ to protect you. You owe me that. M

I had to reply! I instructed my secretary to use a BBC envelope so that her husband would see it and she would have to explain herself. I no longer wanted a secret liaison. I could tell that she was in the frame of mind to speak out against me; her conscious state was such that she was ready to reveal our relationship and bring it into reality, despite herself and her family. But I knew the safest way was if her husband was the first to know because he would put a stop to her telling the wider world.

Dear Marian,

Thanks for your letter but I am dumbfounded as to what to do. Your letters have been arriving for a very long time now and I have only tried to help you by sometimes replying. I have done nothing to encourage you but simply answered a few questions. It worries me that you have got the situation between us all wrong and completely out of hand. I cannot imagine why you have made me into some sort of fantasy. No purpose whatsoever would come from us meeting. Frankly, I recommend that you seek a doctor's advice.

Kind regards,
Jack K

MARIAN

I was taken aback when the envelope arrived. It sat on the mat with BBC boldly displayed on the front and I assumed that Hannah had used it by mistake. I was annoyed by Jack's suggestion that I ought to seek a doctor's advice; did he mean my husband or a psychiatrist? I had told him that Robert was a medical doctor, but as Jack's work was so psychological I was unsure. Was he suggesting that I was ill?

I knew that I was a bit preoccupied that evening and so as not to show it, I encouraged Robert to talk about his lifelong commitment to handicapped children at the hospital. Gladly, he welcomed my manipulation of him, as he was always ready for the opportunity to talk about his work. It was demanding and it absorbed him, but what he was saying was very dull to me at that moment, as my irritated mind raced to make sense of what Jack had meant and indeed what I ought to do about it.

Looking at me while speaking of his patients, Robert

had not the slightest reason to doubt my state of mind. He continued telling me tales of unhappiness, injustice and despair. I felt sad for the first time that my actions could hurt this good man and I decided that I would take a step to further my desire to write.

The next day, I enrolled on a creative writing course. I felt that I could at least give it a go.

JACK

It felt like stalking. I was trapped, so I had to shut Marian up before she could go any further. The code that I worked under had been broken; I was not as clever as I had thought! The work of Marcel Proust had taught me to use my memory and to look to my inner world for my imaginings. As I mentioned, he had said to express the unconscious world would interest someone, somewhere, and I had shown Marian the way. How right he was; she had followed the leader. However, he didn't warn of the price one had to pay for such attention.

The Jekyll and Hyde in me wanted to both help her and to quieten her. To stimulate her and yet to be rid of her. To tease her and to draw her to me and to push her away and to ignore her. She had worked her way into my life with my blessing, but now she had to go. I could not allow myself to be dependent on her or her on me. I had to remember Jung's crystal-clear warning.

My constant aim was to try my hardest to remember his

advice. My character was such that it was made very difficult for me. If only Marian had been able to keep her distance, we would not have been in this confrontation. However, her next letter was a step in the right direction.

Dear Jack,

Your letter could have been suggesting that I am going mad, but I will give you the benefit of the doubt and tell you that I have enrolled in a creative writing course. After all, we are told that Art is the only redemption.

Bye,
Marian

In my feeble state, I felt that I wanted to answer this. Marcel Proust believed that Art was indeed the only redemption. We were both ping-pong champions; both of us push-me, pull-me addicts unable to resist.

Dear Marian,

Thanks for your letter. I am so pleased that you are going to classes. Enjoy the journey that you are on.

Best wishes, Jack

I allowed encouragement this time. It was weak of me, but my need of her was still real. My confused state of mind was a symptom of the depression that I was subject to. I had fought hard to control the highs and lows most of my adult life. There was nothing average about my psychological make-up and I could understand how Jung had found such a good word to describe personalities as 'complex'.

Over time, I had endeavoured to achieve the process of individuation and I had reached success in the literary world. In order to succeed as a broadcaster, I had had to be ruthless; using Marian as a means of creative inspiration had been another step in the think tank. I keep stressing that Jung's theory had well and truly been put to the test and had been proven by my experiment. If I had not been such a coward, I would have delighted in acclaiming my psychological experiment as a great victory. I tried to excuse my unwillingness to tell, as a protection for Marian and her family. However, knowing my own nature, I had to admit that were it to my advantage to expose our mind link, I would have done so.

No, it was no kindness on my part that kept my spiritual affair hidden from view; it was the sheer horror of having my secret code exposed that kept me quiet. Of course, I would have liked to prove my art to the elitists, but that would have to wait for posterity. One day, I knew that my work would be examined alongside my diaries, and the letters that I had collected over the years from Marian would bear witness to both my skill and my psychology. If she did develop as an artist in her own right it would pay homage to me above all else. It was an exciting experiment, so why did it worry and frighten me so?

I had enjoyed the game right under everyone's noses; it was that which excited me the most. Conducting a romance under the gaze of the literary world and the critics and pulling the wool over my dear wife's eyes. The public who imagined that we lived in married bliss and that my wife could own not only my body but my very soul. How little they knew! I played the game of being and seeming to be. I seemed to be a good husband and father to our children. They had no idea that I despised, loathed, the trap that I found myself in. But because I was allowed the freedom that Pauline afforded me, I felt forever tied to her in loyalty and obligation.

Had she bothered she could have found out exactly how I felt, had she taken the trouble to understand my work, but she was a good woman who took my work at face value. Her imagination asked no questions as to any hidden meaning behind my words. Knowing this lack of imagination, I took advantage and wrote cruelly in my novels of our relationship, exposing the lack of spiritual union between us. She was good in bed, I was used to her body, but there was no love in our sexual union. Not for me. Just the need to fulfil a strong sensual desire. But if I pleased her, what harm? I asked myself.

The spiritual union that I sought was fulfilled by Marian but it now threatened my everyday life. I was often referred to by the press as a nice guy, so I had to protect that image. I had worked hard to gain a place in the world of literature and was much respected as a man of letters. I had avoided scandal throughout my working life. In fact, all my life I had resisted temptation; as I mentioned earlier, the life within my head was more real to me than any actual day-to-day encounters.

The new autumn season showed with great deliberation just how artists collected ideas, thoughts and feelings, and turned them into a piece of work. The healing or tormented part that dwelt within most people, if only they could learn to recognise it. My purpose was to explain this. I wanted Marian to learn now how to develop the potential she had shown in her letters to me. The message behind my editing now was quite different – no words with hidden meanings, just the straightforward voice of other artists speaking, urging Marian to train the masculine side of her mind still more. The all-important masculine side of her mind, the animus, required more dominance if she was going to succeed as a writer.

Dear Jack,

Hallo and welcome back. I enjoyed the programmes so far. I have no problem in hearing the music, but it's playing the tune that I find difficult. Try as I may, I cannot seem to master the skill of storytelling. I know what I want to say, but I have no idea how to compose around it. That does not mean I will give up, though. The gift to speak out loud is what I need.

Love, Marian

PS Pinch, punch, first day of the month

We had featured the song titled 'Jung in Africa,' which speaks of listening to the beat all around, then as the rhythm moves the soul, the singer screams out loud. Then the next programme I edited very carefully was about how a writer uses local records and libraries for research. Interviews captured the past, all following a close pattern to the way of life that Marian held so dear from her fond memories of Ireland. I tried to persuade her to embark upon a voyage around her father. She responded:

Dear Jack,

This time I am lost for words, with each season you manage to surprise me more, thank you!

I really am trying, but time is the deadly enemy. The house is seldom quiet enough; it is a noisy household with comings and goings all the time.

Love to you,
Marian

PS A few weeks ago, Margaret Thatcher did say something that I agreed with. It was her concern for the growing number of children living in a single-parent household. It is a very worrying situation now in the eighties. When I sit in my home with the love of the family unit, I truly cherish that for my children. We are very lucky as a family. I do think that my childhood was more colourful, though, with generations of Londoners on one side and Irish on the other. My children are used to a suburban life, which is quite different.

Bye,
Marian

The following week, I took a look at a crime writer and explored her famous characters by featuring extracts from her books, which teased the listener into wanting to know more. I finished the programme with the telephone ringing and the villain's voice saying, 'As I reached for the telephone, my heart sank as I realised that I might have been found out.' I still wanted her to obey me; I wanted to see if I could still will her to pick up the phone. She had resisted before, would she allow herself to give in now? Just how strong was she growing? I had ignored her request to 'grin asleep', so I guessed that she would not give in. We were both trying to be in charge now. I played a dangerous hand, even with myself.

Dear Jack,

You teased me with the telephone and I would dearly love to say hallo, but at the moment I cannot bring myself to ask for you. I think that you are seldom in because of recording and writing. You could, however, ring me!

Marian

Damn her, she would not ring me; she wanted to bend my will so as to make me reach her. I had to remind myself of the dangers of giving in to her. Once again, I felt the need to distance myself from her, let her remain my slave. I would never, ever contact her again. No more letters, no more playing around with programmes. My book was about to be published; she had filled my head for long enough. I would rid myself of her once and for all. I told myself that I really would.

Then came:

Many thanks for your Christmas greetings!

M R Davies

This note of sarcasm was written on a Christmas card and addressed to my home address. It angered me that she should send it to my house and made me determined that she had to leave me alone. I held my silence.

JACK

When planning the previous season, I had decided that I would put an end to our airwave romance, but I had hoped to keep Marian at a distance, constant, as a devotee of my novels. My diary notes from that December explain a change in my mood. I found that I had started a domestic journal and in it I write that my world as a privileged luvvie was also threatened by the woman I depended on at home, whose support was crucial.

It was nearly Christmas and my nervous tension was made worse because my wife was diagnosed with a disturbing condition and I felt that I ought to pay more attention to her as a person. I had neglected to recognise that she was suffering from fatigue because I was so wrapped up in my own thoughts and my obsession with Marian. Pauline had allowed me to concentrate on my career and to carve a successful place in the broadcasting world. She coped with our family without complaining of the terrible tiredness that had blighted her life for years. She only told me once she had been seen by her GP, who had referred her to a sleep study clinic.

She had spent a night away with her mother and they had shared a twin room. Her mother became aware that Pauline's snoring was very loud and this kept her awake throughout the night. While she lay listening to her daughter's irritating noise, she realised with alarm that Pauline seemed to hold her breath frequently between snores. The next morning she pointed this out and persuaded Pauline to make a doctor's appointment on their return.

Apparently, for many years, she had simply been fobbed off and told that she had a post-viral condition and that nothing could be done to alleviate her exhaustion. Pauline said that she was relieved her GP had, at last, listened to what her mother had recognised, because the constant testing of her blood to check her thyroid gland was the only help ever offered and no doctor had ever questioned her sleep habits, despite her total lack of energy. It was with relief that she got a referral and the consultant chatted to her. Within minutes, he said that she was a classic case and he couldn't understand why she had not been investigated years ago for OSA – obstructive sleep apnoea. He arranged for a machine that would be attached to her body overnight to monitor her sleep and to see how many times per hour she woke herself up in order to keep breathing.

She explained this to me one evening after ringing Hannah to ask her to ensure that I got home early, instead of my usual habit of returning home just before bed. I listened as she told me about the technician who had measured her for the machine and who had explained where to place the patches, attached to the wires that would monitor her breathing and heart rate. It had been placed in a bag with a zip to transport it home, as it was too cumbersome to wear under her coat.

That night, I felt very close to my wife, the first time in many years. I helped to strap the machine on and to place the electric gadgets to her skin. Before going to bed, she explained that she truly hoped that sleep apnoea was the answer because she was at the end of her tether from exhaustion and disappointment. She fought to hold back the tears as she explained how depression and weight gain had added to her distress and I felt so ashamed that I had not been there for her. I had taken it for granted that she was the woman at home, running everything smoothly. I hadn't taken the time to even notice her weight going up over the years and I had been far too busy to recognise that she was depressed. I was shocked when she showed me the medication that she was on and I tried to hug her to me, despite the bulk of the machine strapped to her body.

The next morning, after she had switched off the electricity, I helped to remove the machine and to place it and the wires back in its black bag. We were careful not to touch the card that had taken a reading of her sleep pattern and after breakfast I drove Pauline back to the hospital for the card to be read. We handed the bag over at reception, then waited to be seen; it was alarming to notice that all of the patients waiting were overweight and some appeared very sleepy. We were seen by the consultant, who informed us that Pauline was indeed having very disturbed nights.

The reading showed that she was waking up every few minutes, unbeknown to her, because her windpipe closed as the muscles relaxed in her neck; consequently, she was never falling into the deep sleep required in order to shut down the organs for the night and allow them to rest and to replenish themselves.

It was little wonder that she was feeling exhausted and the consultant went on to say that weight gain was a symptom of the condition and that it was a vicious circle, because the sleep deprivation meant that she would not have had the energy to exercise and her depression would have been caused by the lack of oxygen to the brain. He said that even if she were to lose weight she most probably would still have the OSA, because he could see from examination that the entrance to her windpipe was very small and that she was overcrowded in that area. However, he was optimistic that she would improve with the use of a CPAP (continuous positive airway pressure) machine. This she would attach herself to at night so that air could be blown into her nostrils and or her mouth, depending on which mask she felt most comfortable wearing. He stressed that she would start to feel more energised and would therefore become healthier, but he explained that she would need to notify the DVLA of her obstructive sleep apnoea, although she could still drive as she was not experiencing daytime sleepiness. A nurse came along to administer the equipment and to give Pauline a lesson on how to use it.

We went home somewhat alarmed but hopeful. We had lunch out in a local pub and, for the first time in a very long while, we talked to each other and I told her that

I felt contrite for having neglected her. As usual, she made me feel at ease with myself, which made me humble at my selfishness. It was good to focus on her and to allow her to unburden herself. She expressed the terrible recurring dream that she had been having for years, about choking on a lump of chewing gum, from which she would wake up gasping for air. She was hopeful now that the sensation would stop.

I spent that evening at home, instead of working into the early hours. Pauline explained that she was worried about Christmas because she was nowhere near ready for the usual grand spread that she was accustomed to putting on. I assured her that we would check into a hotel with the children and tell the rest of the family that we were skipping Christmas that year. After she showered and made herself comfortable, I helped her to place the plastic mask over her nose, the straps to keep it in place around her head. I was overcome with sadness on seeing the undignified situation that she was in and my heart went out to her.

Once she had her head on the pillow, she reached out and pressed the 'on' button and we were both shocked by the noise of the machine as it pushed air through the hose towards her head. It was like standing next to a vacuum cleaner. I made light of it, but it was difficult not to look alarmed as it dawned on me that she would have to put up with the constant noise and the sensation of a forceful amount of air gushing into her airways. I knew it would irritate me beyond compare, but Pauline seemed glad to accept the help that was provided by the CPAP machine and she fell asleep quickly. The deep-sea divers were afforded better. I switched off the light and actually found it slightly easier to fall asleep next to the constant noise, rather than the high and low pitch of snoring. However, as she fell into a deeper sleep, the machine's pressure rose, filling the bedroom with its sound. In the days that followed, it made it necessary for Pauline and I to wear earplugs! It was not the machine itself that was noisy, but the air that was exhaled through a vent in the hosepipe. I vowed to myself I would pay attention to my family and try not to use my art as an excuse to ignore them in the future.

Although Pauline seemed to benefit from each night that passed, I slept very fitfully and my dreams were very muddled and confused. I was aware of confusing Pauline's need for air to be pumped into her airway with Marian's hold over me on the airwaves. One night, I pictured them together both gasping for breath and calling out my name, in a plea for help. It was the first time I had dreamt about either of them to my knowledge and as I struggled to unravel the situation, I dreamt of a power cut that left them both stranded without the electricity that kept them energised in their different ways. I woke up dazed and disturbed that even my nights were to be haunted.

I asked my secretary to find out what she could about obstructive sleep apnoea. I wasn't much good as a husband, but I did want to understand more about the disorder. I had never heard of it before Pauline's diagnosis and I wondered how new the discovery of it was. I was surprised that her research showed that Charles Dickens was the first to make mention of a similar problem in a young overweight lad in *The Pickwick Papers*. Soon after, a famous Canadian physician, William Osler, coined the phrase Pickwickian Syndrome, as adapted from the novel. The most recognised symptom was, of course, snoring. It was not until 1965 that an extensive study, by a French doctor, Gestalt, gave a deeper understanding on sleep issues, but his findings didn't bring about a subsequent cure.

Luckily for Pauline, only a few years before her diagnosis, in 1978, a Harvard physician, Dr John Remmer, found the answer by realising that blocked airways was connected to snoring and poor quality of sleep, which he named as OSA – obstructive sleep apnoea. And better still, in 1981, the Australian physician, Doctor Colin Sullivan, created a solution by inventing a respiratory ventilation method called Continuous Positive Airway Pressure – in other words, the CPAP machine. It was a tremendous breakthrough in the medical world and patients were given hope by having air pumped into their bodies while they slept. I was, of course, pleased, but I couldn't believe that the machine was celebrated as being a wonderful invention when I had witnessed the intrusive, almost barbaric, nature of its usage. Surely a better contraption could be devised. I made a point of contacting a journalist friend of mine to see if she could highlight the problem in one of the tabloids. She said that she would try to but not to hold my breath because it wasn't a 'sexy' health issue, therefore not much attention would be paid to it. Heart disease or cancer was where the research was starting to be very well funded. I promised myself to make it my mission to seek attention in the area, but I have to confess that my work took over again and I neglected to pursue the matter in the coming months, indeed years.

I mention this about Pauline in my diary notes as a mark to myself of what a selfish bastard I was. I even underlined 'selfish bastard' in red. I feel it fitting to share this now because it highlights the man that I was. Marian was up against a dab hand, used to his own way, who could not allow her to rock the boat any longer.

However, to my annoyance, a moving letter arrived on Christmas Eve, which I read just before packing up for the break. It added to my depressed state of mind; with my nerves in a bad way, it took all of my willpower to remain unmoved when with my family. The role I played as a husband and a father was demanding, but never more so than during that particular Christmas when it took every effort to seem happy and to give happiness to them. The letter went as follows:

Dear Jack,

I don't think you understand just how much it meant to me to hear from you. You were my dream; now you have taken that away from me and left me with nothing. I was so happy when I could just encourage you as an artist. I want nothing more to do with Art or my imagination. It means nothing to me now. Your name in ink was enough to please me because it came straight from you.

Jung and his ideas are all very well, but now that you have proven your faith in Jung, how do you think I feel? It is fine to be loyal to your wife and family, as indeed I am to mine, but why are you afraid for us to continue our friendship? When you ignore me the in-love illness state destroys me. I fell in love with you through your books, so I will always admire you, no matter what I am supposed to do. I must protect my marriage; it was safe in my imagination. Now, I am at a loss.

Marian

PS What good is the masculine side of my personality to me? I feel worse now than when I first wrote to you because I was content with my life then. M.

JACK

I started 1983 in the way that I saw fit to once and for all draw our correspondence to an end. I sent a letter that I hoped would do the trick to get her off my back, knowing it would take more than just the one attempt, as my similar previous letter, along the same lines, had not worked. I tried turning down the pressure still more, thinking that to be the only way forward, so that she would feel ignored and leave me alone. I didn't need her in my life any more; why didn't she see that? I had plenty of women writing to me. My fame spread far and wide and I was known overseas, too. I had a busy schedule for the forthcoming programmes and my strategy no longer included editing material that would spark any hidden meaning to Marian. Once again, I kept myself out of the message, sticking strictly to the subject concerned and subjects portrayed on the screen. The professional in me allowed me to continue to make interesting programmes as I retreated. I wanted to become inaudible to Marian's ever listening ear.

My resolve to try to silence Marian continued, but she seemed oblivious to the fact that I had unplugged the plug and was no longer talking to her subliminally. Her obsession was such that she still felt the umbilical cord that bound us, ever vital to the nourishment of her very existence, I could tell. My experiment would no longer obey the laws of the unconscious and wanted to boil over as the Bunsen burner threatened to explode out of control. I tried in vain to lower the temperature. I decided to dampen the flame with all my might. I dictated a very similar letter to the one that I had sent back in September. Marian would have to see that I meant business now.

Dear Marian,

I am very concerned about your continuing correspondence; there really is no point, as we both know that you have got the wrong idea about me. Over the past couple of years, I have gone along with you so as to please you, but I must insist that you stop. And try to understand that it is to help you when I say that you must find someone to talk to about your problem.

All the best for the new year.
Jack K.

I worded that letter knowing it would be extremely difficult for Marian to convince anybody that I was at all involved with her psychological state. I was the intellectual and a man of letters and she was but the little housewife who wrote fan mail – end of story. I was sure that I could rest easy on that score. Making reference to her 'problem' was my way of saying, 'Get lost, get a life!' I wanted her to start to feel insecure about her thoughts and to question her stability. I had gained a position in the establishment of the UK and I didn't want my psychological experiment to spoil my chances now that *The Show of Shows* had brought me even more to a place of huge respectability, not only in the world of the Arts but generally in the elite of London society.

Her reply by return of post was:

Jack,

Your advice has been noted. You will not be bothered again.

From,
Marian Davies

Then came a letter to my secretary:

Dear Hannah,

I am writing to you so that Jack will know that I am not going to bother him again. Please explain that I cannot talk to anyone – it will just not come out. I do understand that he meant me no harm, but being a psychological exercise is not very nice!

Yours sincerely,
Marian Davies

I was annoyed, but at the same time I was worried about her. I had played God by making other people talk for me. I had wanted to inspire her, as she had inspired me, but I could no longer tickle her imagination without fear of causing her to have a mental breakdown. I was aware that I, too, was very much on the edge. I used Art yet again to help me. In the meantime, I continued to receive strange messages from her. Open postcards were sent to my office indicating her desire to bring everything out into the open.

I allowed myself one last attempt to use the programme as the means to say goodbye. I skilfully edited the voice of Matt Monro to play over the long list of credits at the very end of a very inappropriate spool about the performing arts. No one on the team questioned it, but they must have wondered what it was in aid of, as the words rang out against the backdrop of people's names on the screen. "Walk Away".

The velvet voice of Monro said it all and surely Marian would understand as the picture faded from view. I was that conceited and I really thought I could woo her away with a romantic love song, just like that!

Then, ten days later:

Dear Jack,

As your psychological experiment has left me restless and ambitious, I would appreciate it if you find an interesting job for me.

Yours sincerely,
M. Davies

Quickly followed by:

Jack,

Please relax, I am not after you for a job – that would be quite ridiculous. I know I have to achieve it on my own. Resentment builds up from time to time. Sorry, I am coming to terms with it. By the way, you must have had your ego fanned by the BBC, as you were one of their first guests on the sofa this week. Their new idea for Breakfast Television is proving to be very popular. No wonder you have become too grand for the likes of me. Don't worry, I am 'Walking Away!'

M

I pondered the situation and, after careful consideration, I decided to use Hannah to telephone her and explain how foolish it would be to continue our relationship. She read out a few scribbled sentences on the telephone. I was tearing my hair out to find a way to rid myself of her.

'Jack says to be content with what you both enjoyed; don't be greedy. He feels that the more he gives, the more he will hurt you.'

She tried to warn Marian of her dangerous ambition; the one thing that she didn't do was to wait for Marian's reply. After Marian picked up the phone and Hannah introduced herself, nothing was said except that which I had instructed. No polite conversation, just straight out with the words from me and…

'Goodbye.'

By using Hannah, there would be nothing written in black and white from me. No give-away words leaving evidence of my conduct. Then, when I arrived in the office the next day, my secretary also had a message for me from Marian.

'Please tell him that I do not wish to be kept for posterity. I really mean that. Send back my letters.'

Her response was unexpected. I really had had enough of her rollercoaster emotions and accusations. I had tried in vain to be kind. My family life was getting more and more difficult to manage, too, so taking the bull by the horns I decided on the next drastic course of action.

Dear Mr Davies,

I think it is only right to let you know that your wife has been causing me concern for some years now. Her letters have become full of fantasy and I have tried to be kind and suggest that she seeks the help of a doctor about her problems, but she has not stopped writing and keeps calling me at the office and making a terrible scene. I do not know her except for a brief visit that she made to the studio and I think I signed a book.

I am well known so, of course, I receive letters from many fans and I always try to answer them. However, your wife has been pestering me and it is only right that you should know about this. If you wish to talk to me, do not hesitate to call me on my direct line – the number is above. I am very sorry to bring you this news and I regret that I didn't contact you earlier, but now frankly feel that you ought to know.

Yours sincerely,
Jack Kelly

I remember dictating this in an abrupt manner to Hannah, feeling as I did that I was metaphorically pulling the leeches off my skin to rid myself of Marian's clinging ways. Hannah made no comment as she followed my instructions to type the letter and to catch the evening post. I am sure she felt uncomfortable being the instrument through which my words passed, her fingers striking the keyboard commanding the black letters to hit the white page, like a Coco Chanel moment of black and white. Innocent symbols, forming into words, conveying the poison in their stark meaning.

As I signed the completed letter, I underlined my name, feeling as if in one stroke I had drawn a line under the matter once and for all. A warrant for her arrest, case closed this time, for certain. I had no intention of speaking to Marian's husband, even in the unlikely event that he did bother to ring me. My secretary was left under no illusions regarding that. So, I went home that evening feeling a sense of relief, a fait accompli. At last!

I ought to have known Marian better, though, because as soon as I got home my wife gave me the following message: 'A Mrs Davies said that you have been looking at some correspondence belonging to her, dating back over the years. It is vital that you return it to her. She says that your office has her address.'

I was totally shocked to think that she had actually spoken to my wife on the telephone. I tried to remain casual in my manner when given the message. It was a blow, though. I was stunned, quite taken aback. The vital flux between us had worked again and she had thought along the very same lines as me. The same day that I had commissioned a letter to be sent to her husband, she had had the foresight and the nerve to find my home telephone number and to speak to my wife.

I got to the office early the next morning and explained to Hannah that I needed all Marian's correspondence photocopied, front and back, and to be filed away. Then, the originals were to be sent to Marian immediately. I didn't offer any explanation for this action, but I was determined to waste no time in complying with Marian's request, per chance she might go to the media with her story if I ignored it. Her state of mind seemed so determined and she did, in fact, own them. As a writer, I was well aware of that. I can see now that I wasn't thinking straight, though, because by sending the correspondence back I was admitting that it had been of some importance to me, otherwise why would I have kept it? I ought to have ignored her request and, if pushed, declared that, of course, they had been thrown away. I assumed that the large brown envelope would arrive the day after my letter to her husband. It was in the days when the post was most reliable and you could, in fact, guarantee next-day delivery without special payment etc.

The reason that I am able to read through the pile of

correspondence now is due to the careful way Hannah had tied it together, making sure that the photocopies remained in date order, documenting the platonic relationship for posterity, as any good writer's secretary would. Hindsight and the distance of time, plus my diaries, allow me to see what an arrogant fool I was then.

About five days after my letter to Robert Davies, I received a large postcard with the face of a woman on the front and down her face ran one huge teardrop. On the back in Marian's handwriting were the words: 'I will never forgive you! You ought not to have hurt my husband!'

I could only imagine the domestic scene when her husband had opened my letter to him and what a shock it must have delivered to them both. I had no way of knowing how he might have confronted his wife about the accusations that I made against her or what trouble I might have caused. All I knew at the time was that I needed to end her obsession with me and I understood her well enough, as I said before, that to tell her husband would put a stop to her secret imaginings. I knew it was her desire to be loyal and not in her nature to cause hurt to her family. I was not unaffected, though; in my diary I had commented on the weather, stating that red rain had actually fallen in droplets from the sky…

'Even the sky is broken-hearted, crying all the way from the Sahara desert!'

JACK

I was right, it did stop her, but although her husband telephoned my office several times over the following weeks, he was always informed that I was not around and soon he didn't bother any more. His attempt to reach me proved that my words had caused some concern on his part and I often wondered how he and Marian had managed to sort things out and whether I had hurt more than just her feelings.

The world seemed a lonelier place despite my rising celebrity. In my professional world, exciting things were happening, though. I went to a party to celebrate Richard Attenborough's film *Gandhi*, which had just won him eight academy awards, and one of the event managers handed me a new concept from the music world. It was a compact disc containing the theme music from the film. It was the first time that I had held a CD in my hand and I marvelled at how tiny it was.

MARIAN

When Robert showed me the letter, I remember I was shocked and angry and upset. I was shocked because I didn't like my inner world being exposed; I was angry because I didn't think that Jack had the right to contact my husband; and I was upset that I would hurt Robert because I had never, ever intended that. After all, I had dealt with the matter and I had ended it by contacting his wife. There was no need to humiliate me and to cause trouble in my family. Robert held out the letter, forcing me to read it.

I felt my heart beat faster as the words sank in. I couldn't believe that Jack could be so cruel as to put me in that uncomfortable position and I felt sad to appear so foolish in the eyes of my husband, who I loved dearly. It didn't feel good but I felt in control because of ringing Jack's wife. I was astounded, though, that even at the end of our strange relationship, both Jack and myself had been on the same wavelength in bringing the problem to a head. We turned to each other's partner in anger at each other; the situation was so out of control and horrible that it took drastic action by us both to end it.

'I can explain,' I pleaded. 'I have been receiving Jack's messages through the television set and when I challenged him about being a psychological experiment, he got cross with me and we fell out.'

'You have been receiving messages through the television? Are you mad or what? You will be telling me that you are hearing voices coming through the walls next!' Robert sounded angry and he looked very upset with me.

'Look at this letter, read what he says. You have become an embarrassment, what were you thinking of? You are a mother; what has made you behave like a mad woman?'

He asked me through clenched teeth. I put my arms around him but he pulled them away.

'Marian, what were you doing making a nuisance of yourself like that? You are not a child.' His lips narrowed and he stared at me.

'Please, Robert, wait until tomorrow and see what comes in the post. I found out what he was doing and I rang his wife to tell him to post my letters back. You will see then that I am right. I have been used as a psychological experiment and I'm sorry for letting you down, but I haven't behaved as he is suggesting, I promise.'

I could tell by the look on his face that he doubted my sanity. The hurt in his eyes showed that he was disappointed in me. The more I talked and tried to justify my behaviour, the more crazy I sounded. I felt close to tears and very afraid because I never wanted anything to happen to my marriage. I knew that I sounded like a ranting woman who had been compromised by a respected TV personality. Robert and I had a good life and we trusted each other. I was full of regret that I had caused a possible rift between us. I had felt so safe in my secret world, where I believed I wasn't hurting anybody. Now it had all gone so terribly wrong and I was mortified. I had to make him believe that I was the victim – my letters were my only hope. I had to believe that Jack would honour my request to return them so that I could put them alongside his. But, of course, I didn't have the edited programmes with the hidden meanings, too. How, oh how, would I explain that?

The next day, a large brown A4 envelope was delivered, addressed to me in bold capital letters. My correspondence was inside but no letter accompanied it. I waited nervously all day for Robert to arrive home so as to show it to him. I was sure that everything would be all right once he could see that I was telling the truth about asking for my letters back. However, when he saw how intimate the letters from me were, he was very annoyed and said that they were sexual and he didn't like the way that I had pursued Jack. I said that I was truly sorry and that I had become too involved without intending to. He said that he would have to think it all over and we left it at that.

It was then I realised that without the cleverly edited programmes I had no way of convincing Robert or anyone what Jack had been up to. It had been such a clever psychological game that he had played, like a magician – not even the slight of hand could detect the hidden meaning. It had required years of grooming to achieve what he had achieved. How could I explain that I had been the attentive ear of the trained mind, radicalised by the master of illusions? The more I tried to explain, the more ridiculous I sounded.

Because of my voyage around the shelves in the library, I had made an enemy of Jack. I had understood his very soul and I had been foolish enough to let him know it. It was not until we both turned on each other that I saw Jack as a real flesh and blood person; before then, I had held him high on a pedestal. He had pulled me close to him, made me admit my own nature and then pushed me away. He had amused himself with me and then abused me.

Maybe the great man of letters was afraid of himself; afraid of his true feelings, unable to relate to anyone, except on paper, in fiction. And now he had betrayed me. I became too close even for his scheming plan. It was as though he thought I had stolen that secret part of him and that I would bring him down. I longed to confront him and to demand an explanation of why he had been so cruel; why he had thought that he could ruin my life by contacting my husband. Of course, the famous Jack Kelly had once again been very clever, though. His letter accusing me of being insane and a pest meant that I had no option but to sever all contact with him for fear of confirming his allegations.

I have explained before that I had held Jack in my imagined world. I had kept him deep down in that secret part of my mind, as a sort of guardian angel who kept my thoughts company. A comfort blanket of the mind. And instead of running the material through my fingers, I had allowed my mind to ponder on him like a hypnotic CD. The pain and torment I was experiencing had been all the more real because he was in my imagined world. Had he been in my real world, I could have forgotten him in next to no time. I have read that an affair of the flesh can be a beautiful thing, but soon it can become a mere habit – a thing apart from one's Self. A spiritual affair, being right inside one's head, must be very much a part of one's very being. It must be an extension of the Self, I suppose.

As soon as I had been exposed to Robert, it was as though the drip had been removed from my veins. No longer could I run my life with energy, safe in the knowledge that all was well. We had talked and talked constantly for days after Jack's letter and the more I had pleaded my case, the more judgmental he had been. He just couldn't see that Jack could be wrong in any way. The celebrity world of television was held with deference and those within the BBC above question. The trouble was that I wasn't some silly groupie flocking to *Top of the Pops* or the like; I was a married woman with a family and Robert could only see me as a foolish housewife with nothing better to do than to worship a television idol. That was how he saw it at the time. It was easier to believe me unhinged than to recognise that I had a need that was beyond domestic bliss. Bringing up a family was very demanding and I had innocently indulged myself, not realising that I was being entrapped. How pathetic I found myself; reason told me how lucky I was to have such a devoted husband. That had been why I had been so content to fantasise about Jack. Jung's advice had served Jack well, but how had it helped me?

The shock of betrayal from Jack and the task of trying to convince Robert left me like a broken fuse, useless without any spark. I functioned as usual but Robert was obviously worried about me, because one morning I came down to breakfast to find the following note from him.

Darling Marian,

If your present state gets worse, don't hesitate to call me. I am on duty. We need to talk later. I have decided it would be for the best if we get some outside help as Mr Jack Kelly suggested. You have been very strange since his letter to me. I am genuinely concerned about you and your behaviour is making me think that he was telling the truth in that you do need help regarding your mental state.

Robert

I had made a complete mess of my life whilst trying to be both informed and trusted. I had handled the situation so very badly; justice had been done and fate had turned on me. If Robert left me, what would become of the family that I had always wanted to protect? In my mind, I had craved a romantic illusion, but what was my life about if not to have and to bring up my children? The humiliation of having my family doubt me was more than I could bear. I loved my children and surely they needed me just as much as I needed them. Robert had taken our children away to stay with his parents for the weekend and it frightened me. Carl Jung had encouraged me to recognise my fantasy in a man of words, but to learn and to grow from it, so as to be independent. I knew that I didn't want freedom from my marriage, just independence of knowledge, and I wanted to find a way back to my well-ordered life with Robert.

I spent the day thinking over all that had gone on in my head over the past few years and I was ashamed that I had been so naïve and yet, in a strange way, very bold. I seemed to have been two very different people. Suddenly, it was clear to me; I knew what I had to do. Melanie had left a voice message on the answerphone reminding me that the book group was hosting a 'Meet the Author' event that she was chairing. As the details clearly came back to me, an idea formed itself in my head and I made my way on the bus to the modern community centre where the library was. I was a bit unsteady and I am sure that I looked anything but my normal self as people nodded or called out a friendly acknowledgment. But I was clear-headed enough to focus on my thoughts as I sipped a mug of coffee. I kept myself to myself as I looked about the gathering. What seemed like an hour later Melanie, spotted me.

'Hi, Marian. Nice to see you, you look tired though, are you okay?'

'I'm fine, you?'

She chatted away, trying to encourage me to join her latest campaign and I was glad of the chance to just listen. I looked anxiously around for our guest speaker who was going to talk about his latest book. When he arrived, and after thanking us for coming, he explained that he had spent the past two years on his new publication about a relationship between a hedge fund manager and one of his female clients, who got a bit too close for comfort and was instrumental in his downfall.

From being very tired, I suddenly became energised. I stood up and started to challenge him on how he had sourced his information and asked if he had based his fiction around a real-life situation. I questioned him on his psychology and asked whether he had been inspired by any particular woman. Surely, I suggested, he must have used a muse to write so emotionally about a woman in an intimate way. And how did he treat his fans? Did he lure them on allowing them to be infatuated by him? I was on a neurotic roll and I wouldn't shut up. Every time he tried to pleasantly answer me, I pushed him more. I started to become hysterical and very aggressive, refusing to sit down until, finally, Melanie and Beth, the librarian, forcibly walked me out of the row that I was supposed to be sitting in, demanded that I please be quiet and showed me the door.

'I am not to be trusted. I know that. Robert doesn't trust me; I don't even trust myself... No, get away from me. Leave me alone, I want to be alone!' I screamed at them, shocking them into closing the door behind me as I fell into the corridor.

Once outside the library, I started to cry and it took me a few minutes to do my coat up as I stumbled along, keeping my head down as I walked. It was not until I found myself falling down from above the bonnet of a car that I realised I had been hit when crossing the road. As I fell towards the windscreen, I saw the terrified look on the driver's face. The disbelief of seeing me falling onto the window like a limp scarecrow, out of the darkness of the night, must have seemed unreal because it happened so fast. As the brakes screeched to a dramatic stop, the impact caused me to bounce onto the road, just in front of the bonnet. A young man jumped out of the car as I tried to get up.

'No, please lie down; don't move while I call for an ambulance. You might have broken something. Don't move.'

As I tried to get up, he called to a passerby, imploring her to keep me still on the ground, for fear of further damage to my body.

'Please, stay on the road. The ambulance will be here soon. Let them check you out before you start moving.'

I ignored the instructions from them both, but as I got to my feet a terrible pain in my head forced me back upon the tarmac and the next thing I remembered was being rolled into A & E, where a thorough examination was carried out to establish whether I had broken anything or not. I know that I moved in and out of consciousness for a period of time that it was not possible for me to comprehend.

A nurse undressed me, discarding my torn clothes for a hospital gown, and as she moved me gently back on to the pillow I vomited violently all over myself, making her job of cleaning me up very unpleasant, I am sure. Someone was talking about checking my vital reflexes and taking my blood pressure and I was aware of a pinprick as a vein was located for a blood sample. I was left alone for some time after that until a male nurse or doctor came into the cubicle and explained that he was going to help me up so as to check how orientated I was. He helped me to sit on the edge of the high cubicle bed and I had difficulty reaching the floor without his aid. He got me to hold a papier-mâché dish in my hand and asked me to walk on tiptoe in as straight a line as I could. I was aware that I had to concentrate very hard so as to carry out the task. I did manage to keep in a reasonably straight line, despite the room appearing to be listing like a ship. I was very sick again after the exertion, but thankfully into the object that I was carrying.

'Let's get you back on the bed. The results of the blood tests ought to be with us within the hour. I have rung your husband and he is on his way.'

I was unable to keep my eyes open as I surrendered to the mattress beneath me. I was vaguely aware of a female voice explaining that she was going to attach an ECG machine to me to check my heart and it was surprisingly comforting to feel her gentle touch as she placed the tiny patches on my skin.

The only thing I could recall after that was waking up the next morning on the ward, wondering where I was and why I was attached to a drip feed that was hanging next to me from its stand. I tried to speak to a passing nurse, but my mouth was so dry my lips had trouble parting in time for the whisper to reach her. Much later that day Robert arrived, explaining that he had been with me when I was wheeled up to Brent ward and that I had been knocked down in the street by a car. He said that I was very lucky not to have broken anything and that I had been very stupid to wander out into the middle of the road, on such a dark, wet night. His stern manner disguised his concern, I knew him well enough to realise that, so I didn't even try to defend myself; I didn't have the energy to, anyway.

He changed his tone as he gave me a diagnosis of my condition. The report supplied by the tests from A & E established that I had vertigo, most probably from dehydration, and that I was mentally and physically exhausted. I waved my arm slightly, indicating I was wondering about the drip. He said that it was to replace essential fluids to rehydrate me and that I would feel less giddy and less disorientated in a day or two. He said that I was to sleep and not to worry about anything. I opened my eyes and feebly held out my hand for Robert to squeeze it.

'I want everything to be okay.'

My voice was too quiet for him to even hear what I said, but he stroked my hand in his.

'Melanie was here earlier; she is very upset. She said you were not at all yourself at the library and that you behaved out of control at a meeting.' He sighed a concerned sigh as he said, 'We will sort you out; just rest.'

JACK

As time passed and the weeks turned into months, I was aware of an empty feeling inside and I realised that I was missing Marian. Life lost its sense of adventure without her being out there for me and my work seemed dull and meaningless. I became merely the messenger of others and portrayed them for the great artists that they were, rather than the magician with his bag of tricks. I even started to feel sad for the loss of the attention that Marian had shown to me, and the attraction that I had felt towards her was reignited by the silence that was like a void between us.

I was drinking heavily to numb the pain that sending her away had caused me. I went through the motions at work, being professional enough to do just enough to seem to be in control of the proceedings. I set up meetings with composers, dancers, film-makers, musicians, poets, singers, actors and writers, editing their work with skill, but the thrill had gone from it for me. I felt like a sleepwalker who knows that he is dreaming, but is unable to awake from the scene in a dream. And the nightmare continued; no matter where I was or how hard I worked, I could not shake myself out of it. I had experienced the joy of living when first we started to correspond, with Marian so attentive to me and so appreciative. I had marvelled in being the teacher and her my pupil and I had been astounded by how fast she learnt to follow my every lead. What I reflected on was the open way in which she had told me every time she had discovered the route that I had taken in my writing, as though telling a parent she had learnt the alphabet, so pleased at her findings. A more sophisticated mind would have been guarded for fear of seeming to be offensive in her digging around in my psychology; instead, she told me as if it were the most natural experience in the world and that I had wanted her to strip me bare for her to see. She saw through me with the innocence of a child, proud to show me what she had found. I came to accept that it was a great compliment to be so admired and to be so understood. No one had ever bothered to take such an interest in the real me before. After she had gone, I went back to being admired on the outside but my inner world was ignored. My interior design was left wanting, like a room that could do with a lick of paint and some new lighting.

I became bad-tempered and quick to criticise. Drink became my escape, but it did not make me creative. I managed to broadcast, but not to write. If I am honest I was scared to write for two reasons; the first being that I was afraid of what my imagination might insist on revealing, and the second because I was aware that my secret coded world was no longer secret and I had made an enemy of my most treasured fan. I had, in fact, shot myself in the foot.

I not only turned to the bottle but to the pop songs of my youth, reliving the feelings I had experienced when dumped by my first childhood sweetheart. Once again, the Everly Brothers' songs filled my mind. Whenever I drank, I found myself full of self-pity, memorising the words and all too often singing, as I made my way home through the empty streets. "Bye Bye Love".

I learned to quieten myself before getting to my front gate, so as not to make a scene and wake Pauline and the children up. It is cunning how the mind can coach itself into controlling some things, when intoxication becomes a habit. Even though I was very unsteady on my feet at such times, I managed to creep into the house and sleep in the study. Pauline and I had talked at length about the change in me and I convinced her that I just needed time, that I was going through a silly phase that was to be expected of a great writer like myself. I heard myself justify my behaviour as part of an artist's rich tapestry. All the better to understand the human condition. I actually sounded earnest and true as I made up the ridiculous theory and earned myself time to be outrageously self-indulgent and vile.

One night, I didn't make it into the house; I just lay down on an old wooden bench in the front garden. I opened my briefcase and pulled out a half empty bottle of Scotch. It was a hot night and I was very dehydrated, but in my delirious state I sang softly the words "Dream Dream Dream" by the Everly Brothers...

I woke up the next morning with the daylight – luckily,

before being seen. I loved my children and I didn't want to be disgraceful in front of them. I wanted to hold my marriage together and Pauline and I were lucky enough to have the family that we had. However, my drinking increased as I struggled with the man I had become. I was confronted by Pauline for the first time in our marriage due to my drunken state. Her health was improving and although I had helped her to adjust to the OSA condition, once she was stabilised and getting stronger, I soon forgot her and her needs and rolled home in the early hours most nights.

One particular night, I couldn't find the lock on the front door so I punched the wooden panel, thumping it with one hand while holding the doorbell down with the other. I started singing "Wake Up Little Susie".

The front door opened, causing me to fall through it as I threw my arms around Pauline to steady myself. She stood with me hanging around her neck as I continued the Everly Brothers' song.

Pauline managed to close the door and to manoeuvre me into the kitchen, where she sat me on a chair, but I landed on the floor, still singing one of the songs from 1957 that I had loved as a teenager. I sat with my back against the table and my legs splayed out in front of me, as I went on "Wake Up Little Susie".

Pauline handed me a mug of strong black coffee, but I knocked it away, almost spilling the scalding liquid over her hand. It fell to the floor between my feet. I leant against the chair and got to my feet and, with my face in her face, I sang…

'You did wake up, little Paulie, for little Jackie. I wanta go home.'

Leaning towards her face, I tried in vain to kiss her mouth. She wiped my wet, sloppy kiss from her cheek and shouted, 'Stop it, Jack, stop it. What's got into you lately? I hardly know you any more.'

'Oh, come on, Paul. Be a sport. I had a luvver-leee evening with the boys. I wanta have fun.'

'Daddy, Daddy. Why are you singing in the middle of the night?' asked Carl, one of my little boys.

'Yes, Dada. We were asleep,' said his twin brother.

'Can we join the party?' he asked, rubbing his eye with a tiny hand.

'Of course, come here and we will all sing to Mummy.'

I tripped over my feet as I made an attempt to pick them up.

'Err, Daddy, you smell,' commented Matt as he noticed my alcoholic breath and turned away from me.

I turned to Pauline, extending a hand to her to be shaken, singing along.

'Come on, boys, let's go back to bed. Daddy is just feeling merry, that's all.'

Pauline put a hand on each of their backs as she encouraged them to go upstairs with her, but not before she shot me the blackest of looks that left me in no doubt as to her feelings towards me.

MARIAN

I looked at Jean O'Connell, pleading with my eyes for her to help me out by saying something, but all she did was to stare back at me without any expression showing on her face. I felt nervous and very upset to be sitting in the hospital in front of a psychiatrist. I had lost my dignity because of the correspondence I had undertaken with the famous writer and broadcaster, Jack Kelly, I explained. But it had taken many visits, quietly sitting looking at each other before I let it spill out.

'I thought I had a special secret and that Jack was a kind man who suffered me as a fan. That was until I got too close to his psychology and I realised that he was using me to his own advantage, as a psychological experiment.'

She made no comment as I continued.

'Like all guilty people, I was very sorry once I was found out. I have come to realise that all cheats admit to how remorseful they are once they are exposed, whether in politics or any form of public life, and I had been judgmental of others, saying out loud, 'I bet you're sorry now!' When Jack wanted to be rid of me, he wrote an accusing letter to Robert, suggesting that I needed to have my head examined by a doctor. I hated him for involving my Robert because the reason that I started a correspondence in the first place was to fulfil a need in me that was not satisfied by being totally domestic, but I didn't wish to be taken outside that zone of home and duty. Not in reality, only in my imaginings. Jack encouraged me, nurtured me and then dumped me. Oh, what a tangled web he spun, and instead of gobbling me up, he spat me out, to face the threat of being thought insane.'

I found that I was very talkative once I got over the silence between us, glad to unburden myself on Jean. It was easier to tell a stranger. Robert had thought it through and decided that I needed psychological help and as he knew Jean, from his work at the hospital, he got me referred to her clinic. I was physically stronger after a few days bed rest, but it was hard going to her at first because I had not spoken of my secret to anyone. I found it very difficult being introduced to her and I didn't understand that as a specialist she would sit looking at me, waiting for me to do the talking, the explaining. I had expected to be cross-examined by her and it was very off-putting feeling the stillness in the room. It took time before I understood that she would wait for ever, wearing me down with the indifference she seemed to show. Then, I felt it all pour out of me and I couldn't hold it back.

I tried to explain myself and to show how hard it was to contradict the words of a respected man of letters. I went back to 1980 to try to make sense of the communication that had been conducted through the medium of television. I must stress that there were no online chat sites then, and in using the television in an interactive way we were way ahead of our time, no internet, no mobile phone, just electronic waves through the air into my home. I sounded contrite as I said that I had been happy as a wife and a mother and that I had tried to be good at both. I said I realised I had soaked up the romantic novels of Jane Austen and the Brontes and it would have been interesting to know what they would have made of my correspondence. I had marvelled at their heroes and admired their heroines, who were strong women of their time.

Jean stopped me at that, asking, 'Do you consider yourself to be a strong woman?'

'Not especially, no. I have never thought about it. My family was my whole life. I was innocent and naïve, I lived in a fairy-tale bubble and I was brought up on Hollywood movies in the fifties. I didn't realise how childlike I was until I had a sort of awakening through getting close to Jack and his work.'

I told her about finding his novels and how I had then been drawn to his television programme and had immediately sent off a fan letter, which was out of character, and how I had allowed myself to ask to go to the studio and about our meeting.

I spent many hours with her off and on, gradually unravelling the experience and the encouragement I had received from the man who was a complete stranger to me, apart from his books. I attempted to convey the journey I had found myself on and the thrill of finding a voice that seemed to guide me, both through his written word and in his editing of other people's work. I spoke of the feeling of being taken over and yet the strength I had also felt, as I discovered far more of him than he had ever intended.

We touched on my very treasured childhood and the spiritual atmosphere that had coloured my emotions ever since. How my romantic nature had been embellished by the theatre of the Latin Church and my love of Ireland, which had enriched my mind from the stories of the past. And how I had found an infinity with my father and Jack in their love of the land and its people. How having Jack whispering in my ear was a continuation of the love I received from my father and it had felt so right and so easy. Even if somewhat surprising at first.

I told her I had felt concerned that I might be a nuisance, but that he had continually urged me not to think or to feel like that at all. I realised when talking to Jean, and it was to her mostly, not with her, that I had not really felt guilty or disloyal to Robert because in my mind I wasn't doing anything wrong. It was as if I was in a time capsule when communicating with Jack and only if Robert was working late or on nights and the children were secure in their beds. Somehow, it felt as if I had sat down at a piano and the melody had just flowed. Then, when the allotted time was over, I put him away like a score of music until it was time to practise again. I had felt very content before unlocking the thought pattern that lead to Jack's scheming. Finding out unhinged me, and the feeling of being used and then dumped confused and upset me.

I stressed that my traditional Catholic upbringing gave

me a certain longing for spirituality.

'It helps me to understand myself a bit better, now that I have recognised the feeling. I came to see Art as a form of religion, where people find a place to dwell. The beauty of *The Show of Shows* was almost a place of worship, exposing the soul of the artist in his or her work. Jack is both good and bad, like us all.'

I looked down at my hands as I continued.

'I realise that I must forgive him so as not to become obsessed with him again, in my anger towards him. I just want to get on with my life and try to see that I was lucky to be shown a way to develop my mind and to become an individual. I might never have roamed beyond myself without reaching out to him. I just hope that Robert will love me again and understand that I needed to be just a little mad in order to find myself. I do so hope that he will.'

Jean looked at her watch and it dawned on me that to be professional she had to stick to the allocated time, and I wondered if I could be as detached from patients as a psychologist had to be. It would be hard not to get involved, but of course their training would prepare them for that. No matter what point I was making or how upset I was, she always brought our session to a close on the dot – an hour was given and that was that until the next time. I had learnt a lot, but I still had a long way to go if I was ever to be within a career like that – anyway, my children were still young and needed me.

I wrote a lot of this down in the clinic that I entered after I was admitted to hospital, following being run down in the street. Robert's colleagues helped him to persuade me to enter for nervous tension, because I was exhausted after not sleeping for weeks. I volunteered myself to be admitted. It was very difficult for me to convince Robert that I wasn't out of my mind, but gradually he came round to believing me, although he remained angry regarding my foolish behaviour. The only prescription was that I should rest and use truth-telling as a form of therapy. Jean knew that because I had found writing so helpful it would have a healing effect.

So within the security of my surroundings, I reconstructed the experience that had lead to my shame. Reading back to myself the words I had written, it seemed like a fiction – only the room that I wrote in reminded me I had a problem. I did enjoy the neat, bare little cell they called my room. It was basic and functional and I felt like a nun within its walls. It suited me to feel that way for a time, uncluttered and clean. I visited Jean and we talked and then I spent each day reading through my old correspondence. Robert had brought in the brown envelope containing it and I had placed Jack's formal letters inside, too.

When I got to the verses I had written, just seeing them was a shock. I could see that I had been upset and surprised by the state of mind I must have been in at the time. I felt my writing to be insensitive and ugly. I had not remembered conjuring up such thoughts, but I did remember doing them quickly one after another. I think a bit like wanting to spit them out so as to be rid of them. They showed that I was feeling very angry and wanting to lash out.

I have to say that when Robert was forced to confront me, self-loathing and guilt almost destroyed me. However, anger and confusion were by far the strongest emotions of all. So having the accident in the road saved me really, because I felt safe in that confined space at the clinic and I didn't look forward to the day when I was to leave. When the time did come to leave, though, I felt stronger than I had done for a long time and I decided that I would study and maybe when the time was right I, too, would become a professional woman like Jean. I was reasonably young and the world had a lot to offer if I applied myself. The eighties were opening up for women, so it was up to me what I wanted to make of myself. I also knew that Robert and I had to talk intimately to each other before it was too late and get to know each other as the people that we had become. I felt sure that we loved one another sufficiently to do that. He had spent his adult life in the pursuit of healing others and disease filled his working day. It was up to us to heal our marriage and to find the core of what we considered to be a sacrament. It was what we believed in.

JACK

It had been so final. I had left myself no open door through which I could contact her. To drop her a line enquiring about her well-being would not be in order and I could not bring myself to telephone her home. She would have refused to speak to me, anyhow, after what I had done. I tried sending the odd little remark over the air so as to tease her out of her silence but to no avail. My health and my temper took a turn for the worst and I had difficulty maintaining my job. As for writing, it was as though my spirit was dead; it refused to communicate and I would spend hours just staring at a blank page, quite unable to assemble words into sentences.

I developed a sore throat, which remained with me for days, but as I was unused to visiting the doctor I waited for it to go away. During the week I managed to keep going, but by Saturday I was completely washed out and the pain attacked me the moment I woke up. The familiar street sounds hurt my ears as passersby went about another day, oblivious to my sorry state. My throat was so enlarged that

I had to suck the air and to swallow was painful. As I tried to move my body, the dead weight of it frightened me into panic. The simple movement of my head told me how ill I was and the sweat that such a movement caused confirmed this.

My wife had taken the children to her parents for the weekend. I was alone. A violent exhaustion within my mind pleaded for more sleep. But my body would not grant such a mercy. As I tried to evade the day, the noise of my heart hammering against my ribcage forbade sleep to invade my senses. I dared myself to get up, finding relief in the act of will, and slowly crossed the carpeted floor to draw the curtains. As the daylight stung my eyes, the thought came to me that I must endure pain, hug it to me so as to cleanse myself of the guilt. Guilt, remorse, regret, call it what you may, had made me ill.

A true love had sprung from my art, Marian. She had understood my very soul and I had treated her so badly. It was not until she was gone that I realised how much she had meant to me. I had pulled her close to me, made her admit her own nature and then pushed her away, so afraid to allow myself to get close to her. Yes, the great man of letters was afraid of himself; afraid of his true feelings, unable to relate to anyone, except on paper; in fiction. And now even that was denied me. I no longer had the gift to write. It was as though she had stolen that secret part of me. I needed her absolution. I longed for a sign from her that she understood and that she had forgiven me, but no word had come to set me free.

I was not only alone in the house; I was completely alone within myself. Even if a hundred people had suddenly visited my home, I would still have been isolated, such was my depression. In the bathroom, I waited while the water filled the bath and as I undressed with effort, I caught a glance of myself in the mirror. The face of the man looking back at me filled me with anxiety; my forty years looked far more. Once in the bath, I expected to relax but the warm water made my body shudder violently. My flesh shivered and my head went into cramp. In panic, I pulled myself upright and got out of the bath. I stood wet and naked leaning against the basin. I had to fight against the terrible urge to collapse as my mind tried to alert me to the coming vomit. Tears ran down my face as the last stages of bile heaved up from my intestines. There was mucus coming from my nose and the pain from my dry throat made my eyes water even more.

Feeling my way around the room, I managed to position my aching body onto a chair. It was all so difficult and exhausting; I could have cried from the strain involved. But through this physical pain came the understanding that the real wound was in my head. The waves of depression hung over me, like a monster dangling from the ceiling, threatening to beat me down, and I knew that in order to stay conscious I had to make myself stand up tall and get dressed. I knew how to do that simple thing, but I could not communicate with my body in order to make the necessary movements. Sitting on the edge of the chair, I could see my clothes just two yards away but I could not believe that my muscles would listen to me commanding them to make the few steps. I could not even stand. It frightened me to be so feeble and jelly-like. Then, the whirlwind must have subsided for somehow I must have dressed. I have no memory of this or of how I got out into the high street. Perhaps what had happened in my head had some way changed my appearance because several people glanced at me. I could feel the sweat on my skin, but I didn't have the courage to look at my reflection in the shop windows. I felt so ill and I truly felt ugly as if the fever had turned me into the elephant man. My mind was under ceaseless attack and I was aware of the traumatic breakdown I was experiencing. I knew that it was due to a terrible depression I had been unable to escape from since ending my relationship with Marian.

I have explained before that the imagined world has always been more real to me than reality, so my need of her was very real. The pain and torment I had experienced had been all the more real because she was in my imagined world. Had she been in my real world, I could have forgotten her in next to no time. An affair of the flesh was so easy for me; I loved them and left them constantly, but what had been in my head was a very part of me. A part that I took everywhere – waking or sleeping my mind never let me be.

As soon as I had betrayed her to her husband, it was as though the drip had been removed from my veins. No longer could I receive the nourishment that had supplied vital energy to my brain. Overwork plus mental exhaustion had caused me to find myself walking down the street a sick man whose nerves were frayed and worn. No vital flux left to fire my energy. Suddenly, a woman in her late thirties stepped out of a shop and her red hair and brown eyes made me stop and catch my breath. I stumbled and knocked into her, making her drop her basket on the pavement. Instead of helping her I ran, the fight or flight in me finding the hidden reserve of energy that nature provides in order to run from danger. Glancing over my shoulder, I could see her running after me, arms waving in an attempt to catch my attention. The noise of the traffic was deadened by the pounding of my heart as my blood raced to my head, as through trying to find a place to escape to.

It was her, it was Marian, and she had a knife in her hand. She was about to attack me. I knew that she was going to kill me for what I had done to her. After all, revenge would be sweet – for all I knew, I had ruined her life and her marriage. Now she was going to get me! But as my weak legs refused to run faster, a gentle hand tapped my shoulder.

'Excuse me,' she smiled. 'When you bumped into me just now, you dropped this.'

As I glanced back, what had looked like a knife in her hand turned out to be no more than my own silver pencil. Somehow, it must have fallen from my jacket to the ground. As the woman moved away, I could see that she was not at all like Marian and that my mind had played a cruel trick on me. I felt so very ill. I wanted to go home, but I was afraid to. Surely I would be safer from myself if I stayed in a crowded place; what harm could my mind do to me then? The shoppers allowed me to feel invisible – I was glad of that. The noise and the density of people and things tore at my nerves. As I moved slowly now along the street, I felt a fierce, sharp pain in my chest; running had left my heart feeling as if a long sharp knife had indeed been pushed into it. I wanted to shout out. Instead, I screamed inside my head and as its own echo chased around like a magnetic track of pain in a circle, my thoughts spun faster and faster.

I wished for some physical outward sign to give dignity to my suffering. I was suffering and unable to reach out for help. If only I were lame instead of whole, there would have been some excuse, some reason for pity. The tremors and disturbances in my mind had played around with me for the past few months ever since Marian's departure, ever since I had handed her over to her husband. Over and over again those unseen wounds attacked my body, leaving me now a broken man.

Aimlessly I wandered in and out of the shops, faking interest in books and records, holding them, looking at them but not seeing them. To anyone observing me, I must have looked extremely intent on a purchase when, in fact, I was lost inside my head. There is a certain kind of nightmare that often precedes an illness, when I dream that I am walking down a long, long road that has no end. I have to get to the end in order to deliver a pile of money, but try as I might I never reach my destination. In my sleep, sweat pours from my body as I realise how impossible the task to be.

That morning had been such a nightmare; it was as if time itself would not move. I moved heavily, labouring my every movement, trying to make the hours pass. The fear I felt was alarming. I had never experienced such distress. I remember breathing deeply and very deliberately so as to step briskly away from the shops. Somehow, I found myself back home – home? Home is where the heart is, so they say, but if that is so, I did not go home. I simply went back to the house where I lived.

My condition got worse as the day wore on, my state of mind not improved by the fever that possessed me. I must have slept throughout that day and night and most of the next day. I was aware of someone else in the room looking anxiously down at me. She had returned on the Sunday evening, leaving the children to spend half-term with their grandparents.

'My God, what's wrong with you? You look terrible,' Pauline said. 'You should have called. I would have returned earlier.'

I knew that she would have helped if I had asked, but I could not tell her. I wanted her to understand without me having to explain; that alone would have been proof of her love. As long as I held it in, let the storm go through my head, slowly, slowly, then I could be intact. It was too difficult to talk without breaking down. Words connected me with her, but I did not want that, no connection, none.

The next twenty-four hours passed in oblivion. I gave myself into her hands, allowing her to nurse me. She bathed me and changed me and gently nursed me through the fever. My body let her look after it, but I didn't utter a word. That would have enlightened her as to my state of mind. She talked and I answered letting her think that the flu had caused my illness. On Tuesday morning, after she cleared my breakfast tray and went out of the room, I got up. The blood must have run out of my head. I was dizzy and had to hold onto the bed.

She came back in and asked, 'Why don't you sit down?'

I nodded. It annoyed me that I had let her see how weak I still was. If I forced my distress on her or pointed it out

to her, she would have dealt with it. I couldn't bear that. I
needed her reassurance. I needed to be loved. I looked at her
and knew that were she to reach out to me, not physically
but really reach out to me, I would gladly surrender. I would
have told all. Told her I had used her both domestically and
in a lustful way, used her, used her, used her. Confession
would have helped my self-pity and confusion. How gladly
I would have told her about Marian and my need for her.
Would have told of how I had used Marian, used Marian,
used Marian. Would have told, would have told.

She turned and looked at me in such a serious manner I
could tell that she was weighing me up in some meaningful
part of her mind. She was thinking maybe I was in trouble.
Her look told me that she regarded me as a problem and as she
came towards me with outstretched arms, I realised that she
was offering herself as the solution to my problem. I could not
bear it. I suspected that I wouldn't be able to survive under her
pity, that I would be rubbed away in the care and the nursing.
What I wanted she could not give me, no matter how kind
and caring she might be. To be comforted by spiritual love
was what I longed for, not to be looked after by a mother
figure. I could not allow the open arms to hold me.

'Really, I am all right, just let me get my balance.'

Pushing her away, I managed to stumble across to a
chair. She hovered over me, brooding over me, wanting to
talk. I remember thinking that I ought to encourage her to
chatter on, then she might not notice my silence. So that I
might think of something else, I prompted her to talk about
the children. She welcomed my manipulation of her – as
always, she allowed me to turn the key.

I let her talk while my mind raced on elsewhere. It had to get away. Had to leave my body, float around outside the room. It raced off, then stopped dead inside my head. An immense amount of time passed in those next few minutes while Pauline told me the sorts of things that little boys do. Amusing things they had said and the fun and the joy that they brought to her.

Soon, there was silence. I was helpless in my effort to make her continue so as to have sound fill the space. I had welcomed her voice, now she let the silence grow. As I listened to the sound of nothing, it hurt my ears. I closed my eyes and imagined Marian, not Pauline, standing before me, but try as I might I could not remember her face. Opening my eyes, I was filled with horror as Pauline took the three or four steps towards me. The illusion was gone.

At first she sat upon my knee, but fearing to tire me she slid to the floor, resting her head upon my knee. I feebly patted her hair and, clearing my throat, I tried hard to speak. I had nothing to say. How pathetic I found myself; reason told me how lucky I was to have such a devoted and positive wife. That had been why I had been so content to fantasise about Marian. Jung's advice had served me well, but with Marian gone I could no longer cope with the domestic role expected of me. The mundane routine repelled me; the shame I felt made me cringe.

Looking up at me, she smiled and reached out to cradle my head in her hands. Panic made me jerk my head away, while her touch filled me with fear. I was afraid. She wanted to make love and I did not. She had mistaken my need to be loved and looked after as a sign of direct physical love. If she touched me again, I was certain I would scream. But I did not wish to hurt her, I didn't love her, I had never loved her. I needed her.

Smiling kindly at me, she undid my pyjama top as a nurse would a patient's and tugged at the waist of my trousers. I could say nothing as I sat like a helpless child. Face turned up, eyes down. Shyness made her tremble as she fumbled in her attempt to undress me. My mind was at odds, should I help her so as to get the deed over with? The effort caused her to pant a little and she laid her cheek against me and nuzzled there. I struggled not to shout, not to kick. It was all so unfair and cruel on her, yet from my point of view, kind. I had made a sacrifice; I had not screamed or put up a fight! Sitting tense and upright I could do no more. Slowly embarrassment dawned on her.

'Don't you want to?' she asked.

'No,' was my blunt reply. Then distress for her made me add, 'I want to but I can't.'

'Of course you want to. You're just tense. In a little while, you'll be fine.'

'No, no, there's no point really, not today. I must feel worse than I thought. Not today.'

'Fine. If that's how you feel, fine.' She smiled back at me without malice. 'We have a lifetime together. What's the hurry?'

As I stood up, she added, 'Mind you, don't lose your trousers. I undid them, remember? Go back to bed.'

Once again, she played the role of mother or nurse, guiding me to the bed and tucking me up as I lay my muddled head upon the pillow. Soon she left me and I was both relieved and scared. I wanted to be alone and yet I was afraid of my mind; afraid of the thoughts that invaded it, like uninvited visitors, intruders to my peace. Before leaving the room, she turned and said, 'It was silly of me to act that way, when you are unwell. Don't feel bad about it. I was silly.'

Sleep would not comfort me as I lay stiff and tense back upon the pillow. My brain and my body were threatening me. A terrible fear filled me and I was aware that I might have lost the courage to live. Many pictures passed through my mind as I watched behind closed lids, but now my skill as an editor was of no use. I was unable to rid myself of the unwanted ones and I fell victim to the suffering like a drowning man whose past life flashes before him. Faces of family and friends, people known and unknown to me, along with the blurred face of Marian between each image, as if she were struggling to get to me, haunting me even in my memory of those that I had known long before I ever knew of her existence. The flickering images would not allow me to rest as I searched through my memory, like a piece of film before the cutting process. Nothing helped me, nothing except fear of what I might become.

Time passed and the only sure message that came through to me was that I needed help, but I had no idea how to get help. I opened my mouth and tried to shout but I seemed to have forgotten how to mouth the words. Then, a terrible shiver made me lose control as my body refused to stop shaking. I thought that maybe I had been hit by lightning, so confused was my mental state. My head was suddenly bombarded with the dreadful sound of my teeth chattering. The noise became so loud I had to stuff a large lump of blanket into my mouth to stifle it.

As my body rolled uncontrollably upon the bed, the notion that I was in the midst of a mental breakdown hit me for the first time. Somehow, I knew that if I were not to be found as a babbling idiot I must will myself to take control. With a huge effort, I managed to heave the covers back and push myself onto the floor. Shaking from head to toe, I let myself fall across the room and bump my way through the door, and without knowing how I managed to reach the foot of the stairs and headed for the kitchen. It was empty but my glance rested on a sheet of paper propped up on the middle of the table. I felt apprehensive as I picked it up with a trembling hand.

Dearest Jack,

When you are ready to talk, I am at Mother's. I decided it would be for the best. You have been very strange since that woman rang asking for her correspondence back. I thought nothing of it at the time but your behaviour ever since has made me think. She said that it was correspondence that went way back to 1980. I think you were having an affair with her and she ended it. Be honest with me. I married you knowing that you didn't love me but I thought over the years we had grown closer. You used me once, please not again. Be fair with me. When you are ready, let me know. I love you but I would rather live alone without you, than with you, without you!

Pauline

PS At the very least, stop drinking and making a fool of yourself.

I had made a complete mess of my life whilst trying to be both intellectual and noble. I had handled the situation so very badly; justice had been done and fate had turned on me. If Pauline left me, what would become of the family I had badly tried to cling onto? In my head, I had craved freedom, but in reality I wanted the home and the family that my mind had urged me to protect. Carl Jung had encouraged me to recognise my fantasy in Marian. That fantasy was now creating this nightmare. I was too weak to stand alone without Pauline and I wanted to be a father to the boys that I loved.

Pouring myself a large brandy, I said aloud, 'Now come on, have a big sip, come on, mouth open, head back. Now some more, just let it go down. Again, come on. Don't give up. You've got to pull yourself together.'

I heard my voice as though listening to the commands of a stranger.

'Have another sip, it'll take effect soon. There's a good quarter of a bottle in the glass. Go on, drink up.'

I felt a wave of self-loathing hit me as the brandy slowly helped me relax. It took over thirty minutes to empty the glass, by which time I was heavy with a dull tiredness.

Then, sluggishly, I went back upstairs and got dressed, but my actions were slow as my mind rushed to be out of the house. Opening the front door, I was met by the noise and possibilities of the world outside and unsteadily I moved along the pavement not knowing in which direction to go.

Cars streamed past me and the ceaseless sound of their engines inflicted pain upon my eardrums as my body felt like strings in a racket, ready to break from the tension within. I had to fight against the flashing images that my mind was playing on me. I felt as if I were in the middle of a fight scene from *West Side Story* and that the passersby were threatening gangs, ready to beat me up. I stumbled as if I were a drunk who was trying to dance. It is only thinking back that I can see how silly I must have appeared to ordinary people going about their ordinary lives.

My body was rigid and my feet were tense against the paving stones, as though I was trying to push myself away from it. Somehow I had to command my body to move because it was so uneasy and the sound of my heart beating was so loud that it drowned out the roar of the traffic. As people's eyes met mine, I was convinced that they heard the pounding and I started to cry for fear that I might shout out begging for their help. As I began to sob, I went into a shop doorway and wept. There was nothing I could do to stop it. I had had so much and lost it. That was all. There were many greater tragedies and many greater losses, but I remembered Marian and I knew then what she must have felt like. I wept out loud until I was quiet and calm. Nervously I looked around, relieved that I had been unobserved.

I sank to the ground and propped myself up against the

shop door, my head hurt from crying but my body felt limp, and it was all I could do to keep my eyes open. I was aware of my chin resting on my chest and my breathing became very deep, moving my head slightly up and down as I drifted into sleep.

Then, it became clear to me. I knew what I had to do. In my weak state earlier, I had noticed an invitation on the hall table inviting me to a joint BBC and publisher's party to be held that night. I had been invited to address the gathering and in my new calmer state of mind, the details suddenly came back to me. An idea formed itself in my head as I made my way on the tube to Kensington.

My invitation had not been replied to, but even so I was welcomed and directed to the drinks bar and the buffet. Many members of my industry were present – people from the world of broadcasting and artists across the spectrum with their agents and publishers. By then, I was clear-headed and very hungry so I contented myself with a large selection of food and a small whisky. I found a quiet corner with a chair away from most people and tucked into the food while looking around me. The room was very beautifully decorated, further enhanced by the many successful men and women who were well dressed, well spoken and very intent on talking. As I looked on, I was like a fly on the wall as each little group chatted in harmony, almost like a score of music as they stopped and started, allowing the conversation to flow.

I was aware that compared to the exquisite attire of some there I looked awful and I would probably be thought to be under the influence, but no one seemed to notice me in the low lights. Most people clustered around the other end near the little stage area and what seemed like a couple of hours and many drinks later, Ben, my host, sought me out and reminded me that I was expected to give a light-hearted chat on writers and their agents.

'You ought to come and talk to people. It is not like you to sit in the corner. Most of them came along to hear what you have to say. You are much respected by them and they all feel they need your support for their work. They admire you, too. Come on,' he said.

I promised that I would join him but I insisted that he produce his home video camera, stressing that what I had to say I wanted recorded. My request surprised him, but he humoured me, thinking me half pissed by that time. I walked across the room looking for a suitable spot to be heard by all as a noticeable hush fell politely over the room. Ben said a few kind words as he placed me in the centre of the crowd and a welcome applause clapped me into action.

As if by magic, I suddenly became alive again, a performance in front of an audience was what made me tick...

'Hallo and good evening. What I have to say will come as a surprise to all of you, even a shock, but it is an important lesson in psychology. As a writer and somewhat of a champion of the Arts, psychology plays an important part in my work. Indeed, Art is concerned with Man's mind and his/her human emotion, so please bear me out.

London has played a huge role in shaping modern creative thinking, never more so than in the sixties, of course. I first arrived in this city from Ireland then and found it to be full of treasure, the place where talent could be found and explored. It was very exciting to me, a country lad seeking a career. It welcomed me as an artist and offered me a place to live and to earn my living and I learnt my trade as a writer and a broadcaster. The world of culture was, and is, what I work hard to understand and I have had the great good fortune to realise my ambition and become successful. Hard work in the field that I love has seemed almost too good to be true.'

I moved nervously before continuing.

'I am an emotional man and at times of deep depression or personal pain, Art has been my redemption. It has indeed helped me and that is why I have tried to make it easily accessible to the many. I wanted them to see that it is not a strange and a wonderful thing only to be enjoyed by the idle rich. Art, after all, is of the people. To me, it is the only true religion because it speaks from the heart and the minds expressed by feelings.'

I raised my hand after saying that.

'No, sorry. I don't intend to preach.'

I paused.

'But understand, I feel that strongly about it.'

Someone passed me a glass of water as I cleared my throat and I looked around the room at the attentive audience about me. I smiled my boyish smile, recognising the bond between us as I continued.

'In order to understand my work, you must realise that I have followed many writers and their advice. Marcel Proust taught me to realise the importance of the world within the imagination and to dip into my memory bank and I agree with him regarding the two states of existence, boredom or pain – pain being of the most value because its emotion can stimulate creative ideas.

'D.H. Lawrence is out of fashion but I hold him and his attitudes in high esteem. Thomas Hardy, too, influenced much of my work as a writer because of his feel for the countryside and its people.'

I looked around and laughed before continuing.

'Perhaps also because he hated married life!' I paused again here to take a deep breath and I pulled my mouth back towards my ears and bared my teeth, making a grimace.

'Long ago, I decided that it is not the woman and her child that make a man restless and unhappy. It is merely the situation. Jude the Obscure is very close to my own plight, but I will not go into that here.'

I looked at the ceiling as if for inspiration.

'André Gide was one of the first writers to speak to my inner ear, quietly, whispering his struggle within himself. He described the world within his unconscious and its battle with his conscious life. Then, after my first wife left me I took to reading Freud and Jung and gained strength from their views and help from personal psychoanalysis that I imposed upon myself. It all taught me that in order to go on I must go back, so as to understand what had made me what or how I am. It was a long, painful experience, but it helped me to understand how the child IS the father of the man.'

Someone coughed to the side of me and I had to gather my thoughts so as to focus on the moment.

'I started to become more in touch with my unconscious and expressed this in my fiction. However, so as not to expose my very soul and so as not to hurt those close to me, I used Freud's dream symbols as a means of a code behind which to hide my meaning. It was an experiment at first, but soon it became a habit and it pleased me to play the harmless tyrant as my pen composed.'

I gave out another nervous laugh and the silence of the room was a little unnerving.

'The biggest impact on my writing, and indeed on my life, was Carl Jung. His belief that man must listen to and develop his anima, or in a woman her animus, has been invaluable to me. He stressed that in order for a man to reach his full potential as a man, he must recognise his fantasies as being very real, dwell upon them for a long time and then, only then, was it possible to achieve the highest potential, and in my case creativity.'

I became aware of Ben and his camera for the first time and I wished, for just a split second, that I didn't look so dishevelled, but the actor in me knew that what I was about to say might even come across better with me looking in such a state – for once, my behaviour had not been planned. I even acknowledged to myself that I was behaving out of character – the careful consideration I paid to detail was absent in that live performance. I had acted on impulse, after weeping so bitterly in the street. I pulled the fingers on my right hand down my curly beard to the tip and cupped it as I continued:

'About four years ago, a woman started to correspond with me, admiring my books and flattering me. I invited her along to the studio. I was curious to meet her; no fan had ever paid me so much attention before. At that one and only meeting, I recognised much in her and from then until a few months ago I directed most of my work at her.'

My fingers moved from my chin to my lips as if to stop the words from escaping from them, but I continued.

'That included the editing of my programmes. Yes, I am telling you that right under your very noses I conducted a personal correspondence, a romance in the mind. I ask you what better way could I have had than to put Jung's idea of the anima into practice?'

Someone offered me a chair and I took it gratefully, but I was determined to go on as the bodies in front of me seemed to lean towards me, intent on what was coming next.

'In my conceit, I set myself up as an inspiration to that woman. I was hoping to create, out of my own work, another creative artist. It would have been the greatest tribute I could have imagined. I encouraged her to keep writing to me and allowed myself to dwell on the idea of her so as to reach my full potential. We played the same music psychologically. All went according to my plan, and let me stress that it was a carefully thought-out plan, until she became wise to my experiment and then I put an end to it. It wasn't easy because I couldn't shake her off. By then, she had become very attached to me, even dependent on me, and I had obsessed about her.'

I took a long drink of water, emptying the glass.

'As her wave of letters soaked me, I produced two novels. I owe them her support. My television series has been more successful than even my wildest dreams could have hoped for and how did I repay her? I will tell you. I wrote a letter to her husband accusing her of needing her brain tested and saying that she was the biggest nuisance imaginable to me and my life. I acted as a prat, a vile man, because I was scared of the power that she had over me.'

I stood up and I must have looked a sorry sight in my crumpled clothes and my ungroomed body. I held on to the back of the chair.

'Yes, the great man of letters and of the Art world was scared. I was terrified that I had been found out and that my cover had been blown. And yes, I was scared of my feelings. I had touched upon a very strong emotion that was threatening my well-ordered life, so betrayal of Marian was the price that she had to pay.'

Looking around, I fixed my eyes on several members of the press who were there.

'I would very much like you to print this and, if I can get air space, I intend having this run out over the television networks. Marian Davies, if you see this, I send my humble apologies for having treated you so badly. I have no way of knowing how you are or how my action affected your life. My intention was not to harm you but to silence you, please believe that.

'I live with the knowledge that you must hate me now but I hope that one day you will see fit to forgive me.'

I straightened up and looked straight at the camera as I explained.

'What I did, I did in the name of Art. But it is only now that I realise that I misused Art and I beg forgiveness. I fanned the flames of your imagination and fed into your subconscious what it wanted to hear. I deeply regret having played games with both your imagination and your emotions.'

I waved a hand down my body as I implored.

'Seeing me, you will acknowledge that I am a broken man. I am finished. The one thing that I held dear in my life was Art; the fact that I have abused it has destroyed me.'

The sentimentality was threatening and my body heaved as uncontrollable sobs escaped from my lips. I took a step forward, falling heavily to the floor. I must have looked like a Cagney character in an old movie who utters his dying words before collapsing in a heap.

The loud sound of snoring woke me with a start. I opened my eyes and looked around me in bewilderment. I was in the fresh air and it was obviously late at night because the traffic had gone and I couldn't see a single person walking in the street. It took me a few minutes to realise that I was still in the shop doorway and that I must have been asleep, dreaming. I shook my head without moving from my sitting position, with my legs still akimbo. All that stuff about confronting the camera and the gathering at the party had been no more than a dream, a nightmare of confession; and the truth-telling had been but a figment of my imagination. I scratched my head in wonder as it dawned on me what a lucky escape I had had.

The realisation seemed to give me strength and I pushed my back against the glass door so as to lever myself onto my feet. I could see the picture of the dream so clearly in my mind as if it had been a film I had been watching. The relief that I hadn't given myself away gave me a determination to get home and to sort my life out. I had seen what it would be like to have my reputation fall from me and to be exposed as a callous manipulator of the arts and I knew beyond a doubt from that moment on that I would pull myself together and reclaim my position as patron of the arts and protect my much-admired talent as a writer and a broadcaster. I had been down and out, but going forward I would be in control again.

The dream had the effect of cleansing me. I took control of my state of mind and my behaviour improved immensely. I stopped drinking, started to exercise and I took notice of my wife and family. They returned to me and, as far as I know, Pauline never bothered enough to look at my work for any hidden message – I feel that I was lucky to be spared that. I worked hard but I didn't play hard any more. I bonded with Pauline and the children and went on to become an even more successful broadcaster. I left all fan mail to Hannah to respond to, steering clear of any temptation to correspond with any one person.

I have to admit that I did wonder about Marian and how she might be getting on in life. Sometimes, I even imagined that we might be passing one another in the street or sitting on a tube opposite each other, not knowing. She would, of course, have known me, due to my high profile in the press and on the television. She would have the advantage there and it would have been possible for her to totally ignore me as if I didn't even exist.

All of this came back to me after receiving Marian's letter asking where to send the invoice for services rendered. It had taken me all through the night, pondering on our communication and the events around it. I left the letters and diaries spread upon my desk and went to bed to sleep on it. What price would keep Marian from going to the press now, after all these years? Her granddaughter had flooded social media with a rumour, according to Hannah so it was hard to rest behind my closed eyes. I knew that I had to seek advice from my lawyer later. I felt like a condemned man trying to sleep before facing the hangman in the morning.

It seemed that I would pay the price after all.

MARIAN

After sending the letter in which I spoke of payment for my part in his success, I realised that I had acted out of haste, even if with amusement, knowing that it would be a shock for him to hear from me after so many years. Then, a day or two later, true to form, I followed it up with a second letter:

Dear Jack,

I acted in haste when sending my letter regarding the invoice and out of a sense of devilment too. I wish you all the best at the start of your new career in New York, and you might like to know that I have been a published author for some twelve years now, under a different name. I never wanted you to know that your experiment was, after all, good for me, so I did what women used to have to do and published under a man's name. In fact, I used the name Freddie Turner.

You will note that I have omitted my address from this and my previous letter. I have no desire to rekindle any correspondence. I had to send this, though, so as to draw the final line under what was, for me, a very complex journey of awakening.

Marian

I wrote it by hand so that he could be in no doubt as to whether it was from me or not. I sent it to his old BBC office, knowing it would be forwarded to him in time before he left the country. The words of a song sprang to mind as I slipped the envelope into the post box. It was an Irish folk song.

'Let him go, let him tarry, let him sink or let him swim.'

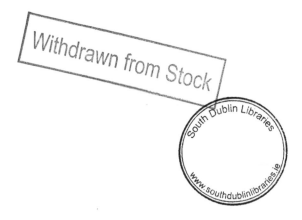